THIS
COUNTRY
IS
NO
LONGER
YOURS

THIS COUNTRY IS NO LONGER YOURS

A Novel

AVIK JAIN CHATLANI

BOND STREET BOOKS

DOUBLEDAY CANADA

Bond Street Books and colophon are registered trademarks of Penguin Random House Canada Limited

Library and Archives Canada Cataloguing in Publication

Title: This country is no longer yours / Avik Jain Chatlani.
Names: Jain Chatlani, Avik, author.
Identifiers: Canadiana (print) 2023053676X | Canadiana (ebook) 20230536778 | ISBN 9780385688703 (hardcover) | ISBN 9780385688710 (EPUB)
Subjects: LCSH: Sendero Luminoso (Guerrilla group)—Fiction. | LCSH: Peru—Social conditions—1968-—Fiction. | LCSH: Peru—Economic conditions—1968-—Fiction. | LCSH: Peru—Politics and government—1968-1980—Fiction. | LCSH: Peru—Politics and government—1980- —Fiction. | LCSH: Peru—History—1968-1980—Fiction. | LCSH: Peru—History—1980-—Fiction. | LCGFT: Novels.
Classification: LCC PS8619.A3692 T55 2024 | DDC C813/.6—dc23

This book is a work of fiction. Names, characters, places and incidents are products of the author's imagination or are used fictitiously. Any resemblance to actual events or locales or persons, living or dead, is entirely coincidental.

Jacket design: Kelly Hill
Jacket images: (paper texture) Nikola, (spray paint) tuomaslehtinen, (machine) emilio100, (barbed wire) higyou, (Costa Verde, Lima) christian, all Adobe Stock Images

Printed in Canada

Published in Canada by Bond Street Books, a division of Penguin Random House Canada Limited, and distributed in the United States by Penguin Random House LLC

www.penguinrandomhouse.ca

10 9 8 7 6 5 4 3 2 1

1
YEAR ZERO
(1)

2
EMERGENCY
(23)

3
UPRISING
(131)

4
PEACE
(189)

1

YEAR ZERO

THE TRAIN PASSES SEVERAL towns and villages; he stops keeping count. Everything looks the same—pagodas, thatched roofs, colonies of bungalows, lakes—and then, everything stops. The dark green forest shrouds the windows.

There are no more bicycles, no more people. Only trees.

At the end of the line, the conductor is nervous. He shouts at the doctoral student, orders him to get off, quickly!

He grabs his knapsack and his books, leaves his seat, jumps down onto the platform. The train is already pulling away, going backwards, back into the jungle. The station is still shrouded by trees, but there aren't so many. He can see above them, he can see clear blue skies and shining sun. His white shirt and cotton pants are drenched with sweat—he can see the hairs on his stomach through the fabric.

He sits on a bench for hours. He is then moved to an empty room, given a bowl of sticky rice. He eats and sits, waiting, waiting. Waiting for what? For the end of the world?

That's what the Professor sent him here to see. The end of the world.

Finally, a rusty, American-made car pulls up on the dirt road beside the station. A chubby man in a checkered scarf and black Mao jacket rushes out of the backseat to welcome him. They shake hands, embrace.

They speak French. What a relief, French! After all those clicks and gulps and purrs, finally a language the student can speak with ease: he took French classes in Catholic school, and still reads French writers in his university library. He is ushered into the car, pressed into the burning backseat, they drive off, kicking up dirt, sputtering into the border town.

The chubby man apologizes, for everything. Over the clanging engine, he apologizes for the train, for the long wait, for his sweat, for the journey, for the shortage of cars—cars are banned in the new republic, we only use a few for official business, it can't be avoided, you understand—and he finds other things to apologize for as the student looks out the window.

"The land is strong." His host nods vigorously. "The land is strong."

Through the open windows, he breathes in something like the sharp smell of dung, but it is sweeter, more soothing. The flowers numb his face and weigh down on his eyes; they flutter as he listens to his host prattle on about production figures.

The humidity fogs up his glasses. After the clarity of the day, everything becomes a haze that he must keep wiping away.

When he reaches the capital, he sees that it is deserted. The low-rise buildings are rotting in neglect, the white paint is peeling. The steel shutters covering the storefronts are sinking into the ground. Bodies of stray dogs are piled on street corners, the carcasses picked apart by birds. The smell of sewage and spoiled food hangs in the air.

His host provides him with a handkerchief. They ride around

the city, cloth over their mouths, and, without pausing for breath, the host tells the student about the city that is now a museum of the old society.

No more gasoline, no more electricity, no more television or radio, no more casinos, no more brothels, no more schools, no more hospitals, no more barracks, no more stores, no more money, no more hotels, no more construction, no more foreign factories, no more factories, no more foreigners, no more, no more.

There is no shortage of shade. Empty buildings loom over crumbling streets, creating shadows that make everything look like it is moving. The student trembles when he walks down a boulevard—it is empty, but it feels full of ghosts. He rushes back to the car as soon as the tour is over.

"It's a ghost town."

"Comrade, ghosts don't exist."

"No, I mean . . . it's abandoned."

His host smiles. "Yes, yes, abandoned. Evacuated."

Yes, there had been a city here, a city teeming with hundreds of thousands of people. But they were not really people. They were slaves, slaves to the old system. Slaves to the king, the foreigners.

"We came out of the forest. And we saved them."

They emptied all of the cities and towns—they evacuated everyone, each person was only allowed one basket of belongings. They could only bring bicycles; all cars were confiscated, all other possessions were confiscated, not for the use of the leadership, not at all, but for the collective use.

He is famished. Even the smell of the rotting dogs and the clogged sewers cannot repress his hunger any longer. He must eat, something, anything. He finds the nerve to tell his host, and the apologies begin again, his host is ashamed, how can you treat a guest in this manner?

The driver whisks them away from the empty streets. They drive down a long road to a villa by the river. The air is fresh, the villa has been converted into a guesthouse. The doctoral student is given his own room. He doesn't have to share with the French communists or the Chinese consultants; he has a Western toilet instead of a squat toilet. The room has beautiful wooden floors, a high ceiling, doors that lead to a private patio. Hundreds of birds have settled in the trees to shriek. He watches the army of colors.

When the city was evacuated, household macaws were released from their cages—their owners were no longer able to care for them. They became wild, careful never to venture too far into the forest, fearing the hunger of the workers.

Their colors dazzle, the bright white around their shocked eyes stands out—streaks of neon blue and yellow and green take to the sky. Their vigilant heads bob constantly, as if separate from their bodies; they stand guard on the branches, and swoop down to taste the water of the river.

When the macaws grow bored and fly away, his good mood also disappears.

After taking copious notes for the Professor, he goes downstairs and eats on the floor with his host. A tiny woman brings them bowls of soup, pork and rice, chicken in chili paste. He eats greedily, he copies his host and shovels in the food, bringing the bowls so close to his mouth that his inexperience with chopsticks doesn't matter, the distance is so short. He burns himself and doesn't care; he needs to silence the pangs in his stomach.

The woman who brings them the food smells heavily of spices. She is also the cook—she works in this villa, she cooks all the meals, and she weighs nothing. She is only bone and pained expressions. He mentions this to his host.

His voice is low, sharp. She is from a landlord family. She is lucky to be here at all. She has the same rations as the other cooks. But he sees no other cooks; he only sees her glance into the bowls as she delivers them. The host doesn't bother looking at her: he only concentrates on the dishes, slurping, chewing, padding on more fat for the lean times should he ever fall out of favor.

As his host drinks his rice wine, the student slips away to the kitchen and corners the cook.

"Do you want some of my food?"

She blinks at this offer. He asks again. Would sneaking her a few bites make a difference? She looks close to death.

"They will know."

"How will they know?"

She shrugs. "They always know."

He goes back to the dining area, they finish the bottle, they pass out in his room, they sleep for hours. Until it is time to go and meet the others. They wake up with the sun and wash quickly, rinsing out their mouths with cold mint tea.

He searches for the cook as they eat noodles and pigeon eggs, but he doesn't see her. Somebody else serves them: a young boy. Even the host takes pity on him, slips him a packet of Chinese crackers, he shoves them into his mouth and swallows them, coughing. They tell him to slow down, he doesn't understand them, he gives a chewed-up smile.

"Where are your parents?" the doctoral student asks the boy in French. He doesn't understand. He asks his host to translate. Hesitation. He eventually says something to the boy, who immediately dashes away upon hearing it.

"Where are his parents?"

"They are probably deeper in the countryside."

"He must miss them." And there are sobs from the kitchen. The Chinese and French visitors look up from their breakfast. They also hear the crying, then the shouting, then a slap. Then silence.

"The children must learn not to miss their parents," the host informs him, as he collects some cold white noodles with his chopsticks.

The society is more important and he intends to show him more of it. They hurriedly finish breakfast and go to the car. The driver doesn't say a word, there is no conversation—has he slept in the car? His hair and clothes are rumpled, his face is dirty, pimply, there are deep black rings under his eyes. He coughs and spits out the window every few minutes. The student and the host share a canteen. Neither of them offers water to the driver.

They drive back into the capital, they have to go see the leaders. The Leader? No, no, the *leaders*. The general secretary is travelling, he apologizes. It's not a problem.

But it *is* a problem. What is the point of coming all this way, if he cannot meet the man who is creating all of this, the man who has emptied the cities and moved everyone to the countryside, the man who is intent on erasing two thousand years of history and starting all over again? Where did this concept come from? He wants to know. Everyone goes to China to learn, and instead, he has been sent to this place. It feels like a waste.

The heat weighs down, his headache won't lift.

In a palace that is no longer for kings, the doctoral student meets the leaders. His doubts leave him when he settles on a cushion, surrounded by men who all wear the same uniform—the black Mao jackets, the red-and-white scarves, the gray worker caps. There is no need to shake hands and exchange empty greetings; a conversation in fluent French begins immediately, the student is plunged into the proceedings.

For his benefit, the planning session will be conducted in French. He insists that this is not necessary. They assure him that it isn't a problem, they all studied in Paris, it is good for them to practice, and he feels at ease with these Sorbonne-educated men. They are quite young—he is merely a few years younger—and they command the fate of millions. He opens his notebook and scribbles his observations, writing faster than the man who is assigned to take the minutes of the meeting.

It strikes him that they are like monks, living frugally, communally, in a palace. But there is no prayer, no religion, no God. There are only numbers and estimates and goals and planning. Rice appears to be the main subject, although sugar, rubber and fish are also on the agenda. The talk also shifts to philosophy and foreigners—there is no urgency, bottles of rice wine are rolled in on a cart, a massive bowl of pickled fruit is passed around.

The syrup assaults his mouth. Everything is too sweet, his head is spinning, these men don't drink water, they don't seem to need it. They are also soft and sweet like the food, they reach out and grab on to each other, they are intimate, feminine. The old man beside him gently caresses his knee, giving him a wink whenever he interjects with a point.

"You can do this as well, in your country," someone suggests, nodding his way.

He smiles politely, not knowing if their project is possible. He *wants* it to be possible.

Someone else is speaking. "You can build, build, build, raise towers, pave the roads, cut down the forests. But man is vile. We have already proved ourselves—now we must remove man from the cities, send him back to the countryside."

"Man is vile," he agrees. "My parents are landlords, my parents are vile. They do not understand the suffering of the Indian. They may be educated, gentle, but they are still vile, that can never be forgotten."

"We marry the beautiful young women to the deformed war heroes. Everything must be equal. If you fought for the revolution, you must enjoy the physical pleasures of victory. The bourgeoisie are not entitled to beauty."

The beautiful young women were forced to marry the deformed war heroes. He can see them being pulled away from their parents and husbands, he can see them watching the execution of their family members. He can see them carted away to the bungalows in the capital that have been confiscated and gifted to the war heroes.

He can see these men—missing eyes, limbs, skin, noses—lick their jaws at the sight of these beauties.

The student almost shudders, but why should he, isn't it fair? The beautiful are not more worthy or useful. The girls who spent their days applying creams and trying on dresses and strutting for the gaze of men should serve a higher purpose, they should serve the heroes who have freed them.

"Graves are a problem, graves are taking up too much space."

"Use the bodies as fertilizer!"

"It's a good point, but too many corpses poison the quality of the soil."

"Ah, well."

They are free with their words, they trust him, they know that he is one of them, and even if he were to become a coward and betray the revolution after his departure, who would believe him?

"What else would you like to do while you are here? You are our guest; you must ask for whatever you desire."

"Can I visit the university?"

The leaders are suddenly quiet. Only his guide responds.

"The universities . . . are no longer operative."

"Are there professors I can speak with? Students? Ex-professors? Ex-students?" He is an academic, after all. The revolution would have to come from his Professor's university, after all.

The guide hesitates. "There are no more professors. Or students. There are only workers."

"So nobody studies?"

"No, no," another man clarifies, "the workers study. Studying is an important part of an agrarian socialist republic. All cooperatives set aside time to teach the key tenets of the revolution. The priority, though, is communal work. We do not have time," he flicks his hand dismissively, "for poetry. There is too much work to do."

There is, indeed, too much work to do. There are millions of mouths to feed! His Professor will have to find his own way to start a revolution in Peru; he cannot rely on these foreign leaders.

It relaxes him, to watch all of the work. They leave the palace.

"Do you produce these trucks?"

"Oh no, these trucks are from China."

"Fucking Chinese trucks, fucking Chinese," the old man laughs.

The towns are empty. The workers only leave the fields to deliver their yields and sleep for a few hours. Skin barely clings to bone on their small faces; they are dark from the sun. Some of them squint badly and stumble. They need glasses. But glasses aren't allowed.

"Glasses are a sign of intellectualism," the chubby man notes, and as the student defensively touches his frames, the host hurriedly offers a correction. "Of course, those who engage in special work are permitted such things." He smiles, showing his big gums and small gray teeth, and the student, relieved, tries not to feel bad for the workers without glasses.

He realizes that one needed to have *had* glasses to feel their absence—the highlanders back in Peru didn't wear them, they worked from childhood until they died, they were born in the countryside, there were no eye tests. But the people he was seeing now, the tiny men and women blackened by the sun, were not peasants by birth, they had been *made* into peasants.

"The revolution is the revenge of the ignorant. Everyone must be the same."

"May a peasant wear glasses and move to the city and work with his mind, instead of with his hands?"

"No! Ha ha ha! No, of course not! Everyone must be useful; everyone must work in the fields. And there are no longer 'cities,'" he reminds the student gently. "They are prohibited."

The student finds this strange, but it is true.

He watches the ploughing of the muddy fields with oxen. The skinny brown bodies chop the plants out of the ground, bunch them together, transplant them, wading through the dirty water. They use sickles, or they use their hands. None of the workers look up at the trucks; they are part of the scenery, the overseer makes sure that these images play out beautifully before his eyes, everything in perfect harmony.

The air is sticky like the syrup. He is given a canteen of water; he can finally wash away the sweetness in his mouth.

The threshing is in the hands of ten thousand men and women—they slap the husks against stones, they put everything into burlap sacks, they load it onto wagons. They are so short, shorter than the Indians back home, and their backs are stretched, he can see their spines—how can they lift such heavy bags, how can they toss them onto the wagons with such ease? And in answer to his question, he sees a woman collapse, the bag has broken her back, she is crushed under the wheels of the wagon, he looks away. There is no screaming, two men quickly clear away the body, they push it to the side—one weak person cannot interrupt the work. The slapping continues, the whooshing sound cuts through the air, as if the workers are fanning the rocks.

There is no mechanization—it is forbidden. The bulls pull the wagons, the oxen pull the ploughs, their powerful feet step through the weeds of the rich green rice paddies. They are barely more meaty than the workers; they are all bone and lean muscle.

"We are flooding the fields," a senior foreman tells them eagerly, trying to speak through the betel leaves he has crammed into his mouth.

And he witnesses this as they drive on, he sees the water spilling out over thousands of acres, as far as the eye can see. Thousands, tens of thousands of people trail the borders, shovels and hoes in hand, digging into the earth, straightening it, deepening it, forming it. If they do not have shovels, they use their hands, they claw their fingernails into the soggy soil, they toss back the clumps like dogs digging through a garden.

"It is honest work," the leaders murmur to each other. Many of these workers were once merchants, landlords, teachers, office workers, small farmers. They had no direction, they raped the country. The collective farms have given them purpose, they now work towards a common goal.

"The land is strong."

The student speaks up, he finally has something to say: "Before the Spanish, the Indians lived together, farmed together—they didn't need the vocabulary of communism."

"Exactly! Neither do we!"

"Well," another leader frowns, "that's where we disagree."

"But the Indians were oppressors too, my dear guest. They enslaved other tribes, they had kings and queens. And they had Gods. Here, there is no God."

"Yes, yes, but my point was . . ."

"And Marx is very important, Mao is very important . . ."

"Fucking Chinese!"

What he learned in France is not possible here, and what is possible here cannot be learned in France.

"Europeans are pansies. They cannot sacrifice."

What the leaders could agree on was sacrifice. Sacrifice was holy. The student had read something by a French priest in a Jesuit pamphlet. Apparently, this Frenchman witnessed the revolution, he witnessed the leaders and their soldiers empty the cities. He claimed that what had been created was a "republic of slaves."

And when he thinks about that phrase, the student *wants* to be a slave. He wants to jump down from the truck when they pass the rice fields. He wants to pick cotton with his fingers, he wants to fight the brambles with the soft skin of his hands, he wants to fill a bag on his back and feel the history of that suffering weigh him down. He wants to take a blunt knife with his bloodied hands and slice grooves into the rubber trees, he wants to peel back the bark like dead skin, stick in a tube and drain the life from the tree, drain the sticky, milky colloid, tap into the liquid that flows in the trunk, pour it into buckets, send it off to China.

All of the raw rubber is sent to China. This republic has no use for it.

He no longer wants to be a student. He no longer wants to be the son of a landlord. He wants to be a slave of the revolution. He wants to go down to the violent shores and lay out massive nets alongside other slaves, he wants to balance on a flimsy raft, he wants to tug those who drowned out of the water, he wants to tame the ocean and touch the writhing scales and flesh, crack open the black oysters with his nails, rip out the meat, the meat that would feed another worker, another slave. The meat that would feed them as they built a new world. And if the meat was not enough, it wouldn't matter; his drowned body would soon feed ten men. His blood would give life.

And then, the ocean is gone, and he sees the graves, and he understands how much they have been unable to gain. So many graves! He confuses them for hills. Flies dart against his eyelids, as if trying to prevent him from getting a closer look. The truck veers near these stacks of bodies—it has taken an army to balance them, and an army to roll them into the graves.

He leans sideways and vomits bile. He doesn't understand why he vomits—he can't smell anything, can't feel anything, can't even really *see* anything, it all blends together, brown bodies in brown soil, lifeless workers inside lifeless earth. There is squirming all along the hills—he can see the workers, with nothing to protect their faces, poking at the bodies with sticks, putting their shovels into the ground. They are making more room before another shipment arrives.

The leaders tug on his waist, worried that he will fall from the truck and into a ditch. Once he is safe, they order the driver to turn around. They hack into handkerchiefs, pat the student on the back, pass around a tin of tobacco. They inhale the smell of the bits.

One man rolls a cigarette and lights it for him. "The tobacco will calm you down, steady your stomach." He fills his lungs with smoke and coughs violently, his throat becomes raw from all the coughing. His throat fills with blood and he spits, the leaders go silent. This guest of theirs is truly very delicate, very delicate indeed.

"Maybe we can go to a hospital?"

"There are no hospitals in this republic," the guide reminds him. "Hospitals are built by men, they are unnatural. It is unnatural to interfere with the health of a person."

They have melted down the modern instruments, the doctors have been executed, the nurses too. All they did was keep the citizens alive to serve the king.

The old man chuckles: "The old society is the only disease that is of any concern."

"The sick are simply victims of their own imagination."

He lies on a cot for days and days. The only medicine available is opium paste. The dark brown blocks are speckled with black and red. His guide cuts into them, mixes the sticky pieces with warm water, massages the paste on the student's gums, forehead, limbs.

He sinks into a world between the living and the dead. He crosses through forests, through rolling mountain trails, into small villages nestled between the cliffs, and the air is sharp, it doesn't merely touch his skin, it bites, it makes his eyes water, it joins with the rising sun to blind him. Even though he cannot see, he can feel the people passing by, faceless people, they pass without noticing him, and he rubs his eyes, rubs and rubs until they are raw and he can see again.

Bare branches cage him in the forest—he holds out his hands, cupping them, hoping for trickles of warm water, and as the guide pours the opium drink into the student's mouth, he feels the drops moisten his dry lips. They taste like metal on the grainy roof of his mouth, on the back of his blistered tongue.

The student's corpse drinks a little more. He is not a body; he is just a mouth, a stomach, a thirst waiting to be quenched. He does not get better, his fever rises until he lapses into a coma. The leaders worry that he will die.

There is no medicine, but after a few days of sheets being soaked in sweat, exceptions have to be made, for the greater good.

"You can't really share all of this if you're dead."

A clinic, there's a clinic in the empty capital. A small staff made up of young doctors was allowed to live after the revolution began. The hallways are dingy, there are no windows—it's a bunker, the leaders and visiting students retreat there whenever an illness refuses to dissipate. It smells strongly of bleach—the doctors constantly disinfect everything, they are forced to clean the clinic themselves, servants are not permitted.

He comes into consciousness under a flickering white light. They are pale, stern boys—they have lost their color in the windowless corridors, they have become sallow and lifeless in a space that replaces the world outside. Sweat rolls down their faces despite the cold air being pumped in. Their sweat sometimes drips on him as they touch his chest and poke at his stomach. He feels them tremble under the watch of the guard as they press a stethoscope against him and listen carefully.

When the guard leaves the room, they move swiftly, shoving needles into his arms, shooting him up with drugs that are stronger than opium. One man yanks out an infected tooth, shoves a sponge into the student's mouth to muffle his scream, a scream that brings him back from the faceless hills.

"I'm going to die, doctor," he weeps in French.

"Don't call me doctor!" the boy shrieks fearfully. "I am comrade!" Then, realizing that he has spoken in a foreign language, he covers his face with his gloved hands, moaning. It is up to the other doctors to decide whether or not it is worth reporting this colleague.

When the guard returns, the French-speaking doctor dives for the man's waist and grabs his pistol, pulls it from the holster and runs out of the room. The guard races after him, the other doctors follow. The student is abandoned in the freezing room, and by the time a shot echoes through the clinic, his fever has broken, the medicine courses through his veins.

"I am alive, alive," he calls out. Nobody hears him—he isn't making a sound. He tries to sit up on the gurney, he tumbles, falls flat on the floor, his bladder releases a day's worth of liquid. He lies on the linoleum, soaked, smiling, crying with relief.

As he rides the stuffy train back across the border, as he sleeps on rotting plane after rotting plane, as he shuffles through lines of drowsy men, as he leafs through his notebooks that are filled with everything he has heard and seen, as he surrenders to sleeping pills and alcohol, he feels the urge to be free, the urge to free others.

He doesn't waste a moment at the airport. He passes over the green tiles and through the new glass, contracts a driver among the Indian porters lugging trunks and selling cigarettes. The capital is the same, nothing changed, nothing changes. Smokestacks from the refineries dot the coast, smog and clouds blot the sky above Lima, and Lima blots the space between barren sand and precarious shacks.

It is an old city trying to fill a space that is too vast to fill, and it will only end up being filled by the dirty migrants from the interior, who seem to live one on top of the other. It will end up being filled, and all of the ugliness will have to be hidden.

And who will hide the ugliness? It will have to be the National Club members, the country club set, the golfers and whiskey drinkers and salon wives who live from their vast inheritances and contacts, the two or three hundred families who swap high school girlfriends and wives, the ones who went to the same schools and eat in the same restaurants, the ones who go to church hungover—if they go at all—the ones who give the Indians a few hours free on Sunday mornings so that they can sit in mass and pray.

They are white, but not really white, not pure white. They are white like the fading, colonial buildings in the downtown, they are whites with bad skin and awkward noses and bodies that gain weight easily. They're really just pasty half-breeds—the men can't keep their pricks out of the mulattas who come from the jungle, or the cholas who come down from the mountains. Since the soldiers took over the country, with their dark hues and Chinese eyes, the wives of these men have no problem jerking off the uniformed administrators. They race to follow power.

Why is everything so ugly, why do they allow things to become so ugly? Don't they see everything as well, don't they also have eyes? But they have no problem admitting that they live in a shithole, he can hear the curses as they push their way out of the airport. They want to fly away again as soon as possible, they will only settle down when they reach their mansions and sit at the dining table and stuff themselves with the late lunch that the servants have prepared. They will cope with the return to their country by pouring on cologne and perfume, dressing up for each other, competing with each other and supporting each other in mildly incestuous ways—they call each other "brother" and "sister" and "cousin," and they all go out for lunch and have reunions with their schoolmates and fuck each other. They will count the days until they can travel again, they travel three or four times each year, trying to escape the perpetual fog that hangs over the sad capital, and they will practice their horrible English and French and come back with patches of peeling, sunburned skin, complaining in Spanish.

He is being ungenerous. Some of them are better than the others, some of his ex-classmates from boarding school now dabble in politics, they find money for a new road, they set up a cultural center or a municipal library to occupy the wife. Some of them take the time to go to a gallery opening or a book club, some of them breed horses or dogs, some of them take second-hand clothes and toys to the shantytowns and pat the kids on the head and then go home and wash their hands as quickly as possible, some of them really aren't so bad.

He imagines emptying this capital. He imagines closing down the airport, grounding the planes, tearing down the walls between the villas, converting the golf course into a pasture, freeing the dancing horses and letting them run wild, turning the British Academy and the American School and the Italian School and the French Alliance into popular schools, or into no schools, and he imagines the Catholic University shuttered, no longer accepting the handfuls of rich kids and scholarship kids, he imagines no longer working on a doctoral thesis that will just become another unread paper in a country of unread people.

It takes days to journey away from the capital to the highlands—there is only one highway, and the mountains loom over him, daring him to stop, daring him to find a different way. But he ignores them, continuing to climb the black spine that cuts through his country. He looks at the flickering lights in the villages nestled at the bottom of the rocks.

The driver leaves him in the town, in the middle of the miserable plaza—he carries his own luggage on his back, slowly trekking into the paths that lead higher and higher, stopping only to catch his breath. The air is thin and his lungs are small. When he sees the lake, the farm, the villa, he drops the bags, falls to his knees, gasps for oxygen, puts the canteen to his lips.

How many years has he spent here, roaming through these fields, climbing the trees, picking at the fresh fruit and sucking until he reaches the seeds, petting the little girls who stray from the servant women, smoking hemp with the foremen, chatting with his father about the harvest, returning from school, then university, each year, more and more distant, more and more disgusted by the people, the land, the emptiness. And still, he eats the fruit, he smokes and wanders and talks, he does more things to the daughters of the servants, who by now have become servants themselves. He experiences the property that will one day be his and only his, until he dies and passes it on to another.

The rain has left a haze and he wanders through it, hands outstretched, searching for the tall wooden door in the stone house, the door that leads to an old life. He finds it, he kicks it down, barges in from the fog, sees the fire in the brick hearth, hears the screams of surprise. The smoke enters his nose; he rubs at his eyes in pain and disbelief, and then fumbles with his waist.

His father and mother—a man of the land, a woman of the land, they own everything around this house, everything the eye can see, they are the masters of tens of souls, and he loves them and he hates them—his father and mother rush towards him, and they stop when he doesn't reply, they don't even move when he lunges at them.

The Indian servants flee as the son of the house begins to stab the master and mistress. He has gone mad—it's best not to get involved. They stumble through the grand house and out into the fog, and as the copper-skinned men and women are battered by the wind, the master and mistress are torn open and made lifeless by a vengeful arm and a blunt knife. They are gutted and bled on the alpaca carpets in front of the fire. The blood covers the student—their son—spattering his face and arms and entering his mouth and eyes. The fire laps at the bodies as he pushes them forward.

He stumbles to the bar and picks up a bottle at random and drinks the brandy, letting the amber mix with the blood. He can't see anything. He can only feel the heaving organs giving out, the angry fire taking them in.

He remembers what he has learned. You need to be a slave to be truly free!

2

EMERGENCY

AT NIGHT, THEY WOULD KILL DOGS. They would find a stray wandering the street, gang up on it, kill it with a club. Then, after they had a decent number, they would put them in sacks.

The city center was always deserted at night. The beat cops were useless. It was easy for the terrucos to walk through the empty streets.

Each man and woman was responsible for finding a lamppost. After making sure that nobody was looking, they would open up their sacks. Using twine, they would attach the mutts to the ancient iron loops.

It was our job to cut them down.

Our shift began at around 4 a.m., before most of the merchants, lawyers, beggars and civil servants descended upon the downtown. We would drive through the streets in a truck, carefully checking every lamppost. It was hard to see—the power cuts mostly affected the oldest areas of Lima, and the center was almost five hundred years old. The lampposts were stages for Sendero's performance art.

We wore masks to cover our faces. They matched our black sweatshirts, pants and boots.

Scaling the lampposts was dirty work. They hadn't been cleaned in years; they were covered in soot. Blood, shit and piss from the dogs dribbled down the iron.

I felt bad for the poor things, but I couldn't stand around contemplating their demise. The smell of unwashed fur and rust made me gag; I became an expert at snipping twine without the use of sight. We rushed from street to street, lamppost to lamppost, taking down the dead dogs and throwing them in the back of the truck.

Usually, a leaflet was stapled to the skin. The red letters, printed on cheap yellow paper, would say something along the lines of:

DEATH TO THE DOGS WHO BETRAY MAO

The terrorists had taken issue with the liberalization of China following Mao's death. How this related to Peru, a country full of illiterate Indians who couldn't locate China on a map, was a mystery.

"The professors really fill their students' heads with a lot of shit."

"Yup. And we're the ones who have to clean it up."

When pictures of the lampposts didn't appear in the newspapers, it was cause for celebration. Every day that the vendors and shoppers didn't scream from the sight of hanging dogs warranted praise from our superiors.

The men who worked at the pound loved us. For every dog placed in the crematorium, they got a few cents. They would have starved, otherwise.

The highlands

From my post, I can see the village. A few huts and houses, the plaza, the municipal hall. Little people moving slowly, not in a hurry to get anywhere.

I watch the village come to life every morning. I'm on a hill, so I get a bird's-eye view. My mug of coffee and pisco warms me up as I see the smoke begin to rise.

I like to be the first person up. I have enjoyed this feeling since school, since the barracks. Being the only person awake is part of my morning ritual.

I only allow myself breakfast after I have done my exercises. I run up and down the path that leads from the hill to the village. I do push-ups and sit-ups on the grass. I have no weights, but I had a couple of the peasants install a pull-up bar for me when I arrived. The smooth wood feels good in my hands as I rise and descend.

The mornings are cold, like the evenings. The sun comes out late and goes away early. I have to use a flashlight as I run. I can see my breath in the air as I pant. I don't mind—it's hell to work out during the daytime in the Andes. The air is stagnant, the sunrays are blinding.

I finish my drink and go to the cabin. I have a sink beneath a water heater. I wash out the mug and clean my face. My whole life fits into this little room—a wardrobe, a mounted shelf loaded with books. A coffee table holding a radio and a cassette player. A battery-powered reading lamp beside the bed. My shoes and boots in a corner, stuffed with newspapers to absorb the smell.

I shower in the stall behind the cabin. The cement floor is cool. I towel off, change into my camouflage uniform. I don't have a mirror, but it doesn't matter, I don't shave anymore. I must look like a wild man with my beard.

Outside, I drape my damp workout gear over a clothesline that hangs between the cabin and the command post. Some guinea pigs scurry around—they are fearless on the hill. They know that, unlike the villagers, I'm not interested in eating them.

I go inside the command post. It is a simple cement structure with no door. There are wooden tables and chairs, a blackboard, some crates full of bottled water and canned goods. I sit on the trunk that contains medical kits and eat a granola bar.

I consider going outside and doing some more pull-ups, but I decide to conserve my energy. The children will be here soon.

THE NEWLY ELECTED PRESIDENT was very young, the youngest head of state in Peruvian history. At thirty-five years old, he was half the age of his political party. Six foot six, narrow and paunchy, with the long hair and flabby skin of a bohemian, he was a failed philosophy student and a marvelous orator. His two talents— speechmaking and being the tallest man in the country—won him the presidency by a landslide.

The president was popular with the people; with the young, especially. But among the security forces, he was a joke. The generals sneered at their guitar-strumming, poetry-reciting commander-in-chief.

"His wife's a piece of ass."

"You think they actually sleep together?"

"Probably not . . ."

The allusions to his homosexuality were made out of jealousy. Peru's soldiers enjoyed their reputation as womanizers. They didn't like hearing that a politician was monopolizing every model and TV reporter in Lima.

The president's father had been imprisoned under a military government, and his party's leaders had been exiled under the most recent one. This manifested itself in a rebellious streak.

Even after being elected, he enjoyed taking nighttime motorcycle rides to bars to drink with his people; he wore leather jackets and tore off his ties. He had a convenient hangover whenever a trip was scheduled to a historic battle site. As in any other administration, corruption was rife, but he didn't like to share his bribes with the top soldiers. He thought he was better than them.

Whatever his feelings were about military authority, the president needed the army, he needed the police and the intelligence services. Sendero was growing stronger in the countryside. The terrorists had effective control over several provinces, and they were beginning to carry out attacks in Lima. If the inflation got worse, if too many rich people packed up and left, a coup was not inconceivable.

The president, like it or not, needed our respect. Early on in his administration, he found a way to earn it.

The invitations were hand-delivered on a Monday morning. Almost fifty of us were invited to the Government Palace that same evening. The short notice raised a lot of eyebrows. Some phone calls were made, commanders interrogated their subordinates, but nothing seemed out of the ordinary. I wasn't too worried. Peru was a democracy by then. There would be no purges—we wouldn't be dismissed without a pension. I found a black suit and a gray tie in my closet. My driver took me to the plaza.

The downtown was heavily guarded, a far cry from my dog-duty days just a few years prior. Tanks and trucks were parked on every corner. New gates had been erected in front of the Government Palace, the Congress and the archbishop's residence.

Behind the Government Palace, I stepped out of the car. My driver didn't have clearance to proceed. I handed my identity card to the regally-dressed sentry. In the distance, past some abandoned colonial mansions and a steep drop to the dirty river that runs through the capital, I could see the slums. The hills were full of shacks; people were fleeing the countryside, scrambling to occupy some sand on Lima's borders. We were only a stone's throw away from them, but we may as well have been in a different country.

All branches of the security forces were represented. The heads of the army, air force, navy, national police and security police. Special Forces. National Guard. Counterterrorism. I recognized everyone from my files but had only met a few of the men in person. The Doctor, my direct superior, was nowhere to be seen.

An admiral turned to me. "Who're you?" His chest was puffed out. His dark blue blazer was lined with decorations.

I smiled, pleased that he couldn't identify me. "Engineer's brigade. National Guard."

A boring lie, but an effective one. He nodded and turned away, eager to find somebody more important.

After waiting in a reception hall, we were led through a hallway lined with paintings depicting the War of Independence. The ceiling was painted with gold leaf. Silence fell over us as we walked through a long piece of our country's history.

We entered a dining room. The table could have easily seated four times as many people as were present that night. The walls were covered with paintings from centuries past. Spaniards and Indians fought to the death just a few feet from the presidential kitchen.

The dark wood table was not set for dinner. Gleaming from a recent buffing, it was covered with glasses, cups, mugs and goblets. There was no order. Wine glasses rested beside tin cups; delicate snifters encircled heavy pitchers. It was as if the staff had placed every conceivable way to drink on the table, leaving no room for plates or cutlery.

We looked at the display in surprise. Maybe we were just going to pass through here. Were they cleaning all of this? It was a Monday, after all. The Government Palace almost exclusively received guests on the weekends.

The doors at the other end of the dining room slammed open. Burly men in suits like mine entered, hands at their waists, peering at all of us. They were not the least bit self-conscious about frisking us with their eyes. The men around me shifted uncomfortably.

Following his bodyguards, the president arrived. His hair was swept back dramatically. He wore a leather jacket, a white dress shirt, jeans and brown cowboy boots. You could fully see both rows of his white teeth when he smiled. Taking big steps, he got to us quickly and began shaking hands.

"Thank you for coming. How are you, General? How's the wife, how're the children? Thank you for your service. Good to see you. You look very fit, you really keep those recruits in shape, don't you? I need to lose some weight, you're making me feel bad . . ."

He disarmed all of us, just as the guards at the back entrance had collected our pistols. There were no more grim faces, no more derogatory jokes. Everyone was enjoying his attention. He towered over the tallest man, making the squeezing of shoulders seem like an art form.

After the pleasantries were out of the way, he clapped his hands together and pointed at the table.

"There will be no business today. No discussion about the war on terrorism. No bad-mouthing of the Chileans or the Bolivians."

"You all work very hard . . . I, like the country, am eternally grateful for your service." His eyes twinkled. Did I detect a sarcastic smile?

"So, as the commander-in-chief, I decided to arrange an evening of relaxation."

He clapped his hands again. Waiters filed in from the kitchen, stepping around the bodyguards. They were all forcing smiles; they looked tired. Instead of carrying trays, they were carrying bottles, one in each hand. Whiskey. Vodka. Gin. Pisco. Beer. Grappa. Wine. No two bottles looked the same.

"Welcome to the obstacle course," the president laughed. He snapped his fingers. The waiters stood on the chairs, and, overlooking the rows of glasses, began to pour the alcohol. None of us said a word as we watched them drain every bottle into every glass, mixing alcohols together, pouring Argentinian red and Cuban rum into the same cup. The drizzles of amber-colored liquid rippled through the air, creating the effect of a shimmering cascade under the orange light of the chandeliers.

Nobody wanted to interrupt the sound. It was beautiful—like a coffee machine releasing bubbling liquid into an espresso cup, but multiplied into different pitches as the dozens of liquors slapped against the bottoms of each vessel.

The waiters emptied all the bottles, departed and returned with another assortment. Again, they stood on the chairs and poured, holding out their arms delicately, tipping the bottles with the precise wrists of experts. They did it one more time, and then they left for good.

"Who wants to start?" the president shouted. Nobody moved.

"What are the rules?" Lima's police chief asked. He was an older man. His tongue flicked out of his mouth to taste the sweat from his moustache.

"The rules are simple. Each man drinks from a cup. When he finishes a drink, the cup becomes his obstacle. He keeps it in his hands as he moves on to another drink. Each empty glass is worth one point."

"If you fall over," the president winked, "you are disqualified.

If you drop a cup, you aren't allowed to pick it up again. Whoever has the most cups at the end is the winner of the obstacle course."

Some of the men hooted. A general, a particularly avid critic of the president, slapped his host's arm happily. "Very neat."

"Of course, I will participate." The president took off his leather jacket and passed it to a bodyguard. He rolled up his sleeves. I led the applause.

"Three . . . two . . . one . . . begin!"

There was a mad rush for the table. Some men held two glasses to their lips at once and chugged. Others were more cautious, carefully selecting what they would pick up first. Soon, the sound of gagging echoed through the dining room—everything tasted disgusting as it mixed together. Nobody had the advantage of going for their drink of choice. There was no pleasure; there was only consumption.

I had a few drinks. I collected a few glasses, holding them to my chest with my left arm. But I had no urge to compete. I could see the army, navy and air force men watching each other, keeping score, cursing whenever they shattered a glass. These were drinking men; they spent much of their lives in the barracks with nothing but the company of alcohol. They fought over women, but more than that, they fought over who could drink the most, who was the most macho, who could hold his booze like a champion.

Part of my job was to watch. I watched who drank what. I watched how much they drank; I noted how carefully or how carelessly they drank. Taking mental notes, I got an idea of who was sincerely competitive, who was a follower, who genuinely wanted to like the president, who simply wanted to beat him. Most of my job consisted of memory and judgment. The rest consisted of the study of people.

The president walked around the table at a leisurely pace. He picked up a cup, sniffed it, drank it slowly in one long gulp. His arms were enormous—he soon had five cups, ten cups, fifteen cups. He put wine glasses in pitchers; he stacked empty goblets into a tower. He drank steadily, paying no attention to the progress of the others. He created his own pace and stuck to it.

Soon, more and more glasses began to shatter, spraying liquid across the marble floors. The men were laughing, hiccupping, yelling. The admiral who had spoken to me fell on his face. One of the bodyguards helped him into a chair. His nose was bleeding. An air force officer laughed at him, before slipping and falling down as well. Some of the generals and police chiefs stood against the table, balancing what they had collected, too tipsy to move. A security officer was throwing up in the corner. The vomit splattered a bodyguard's shoes.

The commander of the National Guard loudly announced that the president had won. Those of us who were still conscious let out a cheer. We let the glasses fall on the table and gave him a round of applause that never seemed to end. He smiled, his face sweaty and red. His long black hair was now disheveled; the gel had dripped down his neck. With the help of his bodyguards, he placed the cups down. A chorus of voices counted each point.

ONE. TWO. THREE.

EIGHTEEN. NINETEEN. TWENTY.

TWENTY-ONE. TWENTY-TWO. TWENTY-THREE.

Some shot glasses tumbled out of a bigger glass. "Holy shit," someone murmured. Others shook their heads in awe.

"Thirty-three points," the president belched. He was holding the back of a chair. His bodyguards were watching him carefully, only inches away. They were expecting a collapse that never came.

"Ok, you sons of bitches. Who's ready to eat?"

—

For more than a decade, Peru had two presidents at the same time. There was the democratically elected one, who got to live in the Government Palace, wear the red-and-white sash, give interviews on television. Then, there was the other one; the one nobody had seen, the one we were trying to find.

Abimael Guzmán was a philosophy professor, an ugly little man born in Arequipa. He wrote his dissertation on Kant, studied in China and France, toured Pol Pot's Cambodia, and became a lecturer at the University of Huamanga, a miserable public college in the province of Ayacucho. Far away from the capital, nestled in an education faculty deep in the Andes, he declared himself the leader of a revolution. Peru, he told his awed, penniless students, would return to the time of the Inca, with a communist twist. His *nom de guerre* was President Gonzalo, and his movement was Sendero Luminoso, the Shining Path.

His students ambushed policemen, taking their weapons. They invaded farms, told the peasants to burn their animals and pay them taxes. When they met resistance, they killed, raped and beheaded. They took the children with them—the people's army needed to grow, the Shining Path had to be widened.

When we reached these villages, when we got there by boat, by jeep, sometimes by helicopter, all we got were tears and silence. I hadn't seen this before. It was worse than the military government, worse than the mudslides that carried away whole generations. They looked at us like aliens. They told us nothing.

"Ma'am, where are your children? Mother, talk to me, I am like your son. We are here to help you. Please, tell us what happened, tell us what you saw."

They wouldn't talk to us in the presence of the soldiers. We sent them away. Still, nothing.

The Indians were convinced that the cameras would steal their souls. They moaned when they saw us snapping pictures. We had no choice. Nobody would have believed us if we didn't have proof of the bodies and ashes.

The soldiers, young draftees from the coast, brought us highlanders to interrogate. We spoke to them in Spanish, in Quechua, we even had an agent who spoke Aymara. We spoke to them with rope, with batons, with our fists. Nobody said anything. They barely screamed. Tears just rolled down their faces.

President Gonzalo inspired much more loyalty than the men who had lived in the Government Palace. His disciples lost limbs for him; they got blown up with dynamite, they were hung from ceilings in our temporary offices. They read everything he gave them: they could recite his assigned passages on Mao, Lenin, Stalin and Marx by heart. They lectured the peasants about the class struggle on his behalf. These children of clerks, artisans and farmers, these skinny twigs from the mountains, they were followers like we had never seen before. We couldn't understand their devotion. This just made things more frustrating.

The peasants were terrified of President Gonzalo. On the rare chance that we got them to talk, they told us that we would never find him. The Indian squatters in Lima said the same thing. My contemporaries all had different opinions on the subject—Guzmán was in France, in Bolivia, in the jungle. The propaganda paintings showed him as a mythical being. He was a teacher presiding over a classroom, ten feet tall, always drawn wearing glasses, surrounded by books and weapons.

In the province of Apurímac, an old man spoke. All the young men in his village had been killed or had departed for the capital. The women kept their children locked up. There was no water, no electricity, no food. He was dying alone in his hut. I gave him some water and rice. The gnats wouldn't leave him alone. I shooed them away and listened to him.

"He is like the rain . . . it falls whenever it chooses. He is like the snake that you see on the path, quickly, before it slithers away."

"Maybe he is a God. He could be. How would we know?"

People's Aid was housed in a converted mansion in San Isidro, the most exclusive district in Lima. The multimillion-dollar property was in the hands of an association. It was impossible for us to prove who exactly owned it.

Ostensibly, the NGO's mandate was to ease the suffering of the internal conflict. People's Aid distributed food and medicine in the slums and sent warm clothes to the interior. The group also provided free legal aid and medical treatment to victims of the state's crimes. Whenever the leftist parliamentarians hauled out battered Indians to denounce the president, the army, or the major political parties, People's Aid was in the background. Every congressman and senator from the Communist Party, the Socialist Party, the Land and Dignity Party and the Workers' Party received tactical support. People's Aid essentially owned one-fifth of the government.

The neighborhood council made a strong effort to shut it down. They put a zoning case before the courts—in this particular section of San Isidro, far from the banks and stores, only houses were permitted. An NGO did not have the right to operate in a residential area, plain and simple.

We assumed that the judges would rule in favor of the council— it was full of San Isidro's richest residents, some of the most powerful people in the country. I was impressed by their organization—they were going to make our job a lot easier.

But the case was rejected. San Isidro was in an uproar. I made a call to my man at the superior court—who was the judge that gave the ruling? What was his argument?

It turned out that the judge had deep ties to Peru's School of Lawyers. And the School of Lawyers, throughout the eighties and into the nineties, strongly supported all "peaceful" organizations like People's Aid, even if they were loosely tied to Sendero. This humanistic tolerance was essential to the School's reputation abroad. The defense of all NGOs related to human rights brought them legitimacy and money from around the world.

The ruling affirmed that as long as People's Aid didn't make disruptive noise in violation of the municipality's bylaws, operations could proceed. It was not a "commercial" establishment—it was a humanitarian one.

I understood and hung up. The School of Lawyers was too big an opponent to tackle. All of the country's sixty thousand advocates had to pay dues to the School each month if they wanted to keep practicing law. This arrangement, a holdover from the nineteenth century, was a deterrent to any attacks. They had the best lawyers, shitloads of money and contacts at the UN. People's Aid was staying put.

We kept surveillance on the property at all times, twenty-four hours a day, seven days a week. We had a car across the street and a car around the back. People's Aid probably knew of us—it's hard to keep up surveillance for years without being noticed. Still, we compiled files full of pictures, names, dates, times. Lawyers. Judges. Professors. Students. Union leaders. Journalists. Doctors. All of them wearing nice clothes, carrying nice bags. Some came by foot, but a lot of them drove late-model cars. Some even had chauffeurs. Their solidarity with the poor ran deep.

The Shining Path relied on People's Aid for surgeons and legal support. The NGO gave the terrorists access to a wide array of contacts in the judiciary, the public universities and the unions. It was an open secret that without the funds from People's Aid, the terrucos would be completely dependent on drug trafficking and bank robberies.

Guzmán needed a foothold in the city; he needed supporters to fill the ranks of his movement from all walks of life, he needed an ideological awakening among the students, the workers, the intelligentsia. When the Shining Path had finally conquered the countryside and shot its way into Lima, there would be a shadow government ready and waiting to take control of Peru.

I never slept well in those years. I used to take the dawn shift outside of the San Isidro mansion, sit in the car and have some coffee with a member of my team. It was easy for me to make the 4 a.m. turnover. Surveilling People's Aid was the most relaxing part of my job.

Dawn to late morning was the busiest time for the NGO. Trying to be discreet, playing the role of subversives, the yawning men and women would be let in at the gate, and step inside the thick wooden doors of the house. San Isidro had good lighting. Everything ran on generators. We could see the faces clearly; the pictures we took were of excellent quality.

Hardly anyone who strolled into People's Aid was much to look at. The men, usually sporting beards and long hair, had thin arms and soft bellies. The women were either chunky or extremely thin—there was nothing alluring about them. Everyone walked awkwardly. I bet none of them had ever played a sport. We could have killed them all without drawing a weapon or breaking a sweat.

Beside People's Aid, there was a small apartment building. The eight elegant units were old, built from stone. A weeping willow obscured the balconies. The tenants were mostly elderly; they rose early to walk their dogs. A couple even put their cat on a harness and strolled through the neighborhood before breakfast.

These rich old people had survived the military government and the agrarian reform, and they would survive the bombings that frequently erupted just a few blocks away.

As far as I could tell, only one tenant wasn't elderly. He was in his late forties. He was a bit famous, actually. A writer. He wasn't affiliated with People's Aid—he never went inside the mansion—but I kept an eye on him, just in case.

Sometimes, in the early morning, the security guard to his building would open the door for him and his girlfriend. She was a beautiful young woman. She had wheat-colored skin and delicate curves. Her dresses were pastel-colored; her coats were blue and hugged her body tightly.

She didn't match him. He was at least twenty years older. His pale face was weathered, while hers was smooth and full. His long black hair was curly, with streaks of silvery gray—he didn't make an effort to groom. Her brown hair was well below her shoulders, always carefully brushed and straightened.

There was a tired smile on her face when she left at dawn. She would kiss him goodbye before sliding into the taxi. A tuck of the hair behind her ears, a kind word to the driver. A touch of pale rose lipstick. An adjustment of the fabrics that modestly covered her breasts.

He would stand on the stoop, watching her. When the car departed, his eyes would follow it for a moment, and then he would go back inside, back to bed.

I used to wonder if she loved him.

—

The smell of dead fish hovers over the coast. As you drive up and down the highway that runs between Chile and Ecuador, you cannot escape that smell. It doesn't matter how fast you drive, how many oil refineries you pass. The smell of mackerel and tilapia spoiling on the beach will penetrate the thickest car window.

We used to hop on buses that made trips along the coast. In Lima, students would hop on the jitneys and shout slogans, pass around leaflets, but beyond the capital, hijackings were common. On the buses that traveled through the provinces, two or three of us would take different seats and wait. Whenever we reached a town without incident, we would tell the driver to let us off. We'd get on another bus, waiting, hoping for an attack. If we couldn't find the terrucos, they'd have to find us.

Outside of Ica, a desert town, the bus began to slow down. Everyone heard the driver curse. The women began to cry. A few people crossed themselves. I turned in my seat—I was near the front—and made eye contact with Ramfis and Jair. They looked eager.

The bus grinded to a halt, jolting as it went over some bumps in the road. I leaned over the woman beside me to get a look out the window. There were three or four young men. Boys, really. They had rolled some rocks onto the highway.

I heard the wheels screech against the sand on the road. The driver was changing gears, judging to see if he could turn around. He had to be careful—if he went off the narrow highway, he'd be stuck in the rocks. The old bus wouldn't be able to handle the terrain.

If Senderistas stopped a bus, it was rare that they would kill every passenger. They preferred to execute a few and send the rest on their way. It was a powerful fear tactic to dissuade people from traveling. Guzmán's ultimate goal was to cut Lima off from the rest of the country, stopping the peasants from trying to reach the capital.

I got out of my seat. Holding the bars of the luggage racks to stabilize myself, I walked up to the driver. I looked around carefully—aside from Ramfis and Jair, nobody seemed calm. This was good; it meant that there were no terrucos on the bus.

"Don't turn around. I'm a policeman. I'll handle this. Just open the door when they want to come inside."

He looked up at me in distress—I couldn't tell if he had processed a word. Finally, his terrified face shut down. He cut the engine.

The tears and moaning didn't stop. I walked back to my seat, sitting down just as a terruco began to bang on the door. The driver popped it open.

Two men boarded. They were short and skinny with dark, dirt-covered skin. Wool knit caps covered their hair. Bloodshot eyes squinted at us. They wore sweatpants and layers of fleece, looking more like hitchhikers than terrorists.

It was getting dark outside—the desert got cold at night. I felt the coolness of the Beretta on my waist—it was a new model, still officially off the market. The Italians, at the request of our CIA friends, had sent us an early shipment.

The metal felt invigorating against my skin.

"You are traveling through liberated territory. The glorious Shining Path has freed this land from an illegitimate state. The Marxist people's revolution is underway."

He droned on loudly, giving the speech he gave dozens of times each day. His comrade had his hands folded behind his back. Neither of them pulled out any weapons. Two more boys waited outside. I couldn't see if they were carrying anything.

"President Gonzalo is leading the proletariat towards a new future. The oppression has ceased in the countryside. Now the Peruvian people must stand against the oppression of the bourgeoisie in the cities."

He seemed oblivious to the fact that nobody was looking at him. The crying was louder now; a baby girl was shrieking at the top of her lungs. Some chickens in a cage had woken up and were clucking like mad. Children and animals—they know when evil is upon them.

"Exit in an orderly fashion. If you resist, you will be punished under the popular authority of the people's courts."

Nobody hesitated. The bus driver stood, followed by all of the passengers. I stood up as well, and so did my men. We began to file out of the bus.

"Please, please don't make me move my children." A woman pleaded with the terrucos in Quechua. She had a baby on her back, a baby in her arms. A little boy was clinging to her legs. The hijackers stared at her, unresponsive to her questions. She switched to Spanish, asking for mercy.

Suddenly, the silent young man's hand shot out. He slapped her in the face. The little boy screamed. The woman stumbled, but didn't drop her babies. Pacified, she left the bus without another word, her children wailing as they stepped out into the desert.

I kept calm. I didn't react. As I passed the terrucos to leave the bus, I could feel their eyes watching me. Too tall for an Indian, I stood out among the passengers. For such young boys, they were very observant.

I shivered from the cold and the adrenaline as I stood with the group. The two terrucos waiting outside were carrying metal pipes. One of them also had an old rifle flung over his shoulder.

Ramfis was a paratrooper before he joined SIN—Servicio de Inteligencia Nacional del Perú. The entirety of his gym-built body was tense as he rocked on his feet in the sand. His eyes were on the bus door. He smiled when the two terrucos jumped down and joined the rest of their troop.

The same young man who had spoken on the bus began talking again. He appeared to be the leader. "Hand over all documents and currency. If you are carrying valuables, hand them over as well. These are donations for the people's war."

The oldest of the four, a mestizo with a hooked nose, handed his metal pipe to the man with the rifle. Slowly, he went from person to person. He would look at the identity card, hand it back, and accept bills, a watch, a chain. He didn't look nervous, and his hands didn't shake as he made each transaction.

He reached me, a scowl on his face. I towered over him. My shoulders were broader. I gave him a winning smile as I handed over my identity card.

"Good evening," I said.

As he looked at the lamination, I shot him in the stomach.

The sound broke the silence of the desert. The passengers screamed and ducked down, hands covering their ears and heads. Years of car bombs and assassinations had taught them well.

Jair shot the man carrying the rifle in the shoulder. Ramfis and I moved in towards the leader and his silent deputy, guns held out in front of us.

"Get on your knees, put your hands behind your heads. Slowly, slowly."

They obeyed. Ramfis and Jair stood over them. Jair, a discharged detective, was breathing heavily. He lowered his gun to pop some chewing tobacco into his mouth.

The man with the rifle was lying on the ground. Blood was pouring out of his shoulder into the sand.

I spoke to the passengers.

"Please get back on the bus. You're safe now." The driver came up to me, blubbering his gratitude.

"Get back on the bus, sir. Don't start the engine. We'll be with you soon."

The children were still crying, but the adults were now calm. They scrambled to get back to their seats.

I weighed the Beretta in my hand as I looked down at our prisoners.

"Where are you from?"

No answer.

Ramfis chuckled. "Not so talkative now, eh?"

I moved to the other man. He stared at my knees, hatred seeping from his eyes.

"Are you a soldier for the revolution?"

His eyes flickered up at me.

"Yes." His voice was soft, almost lost in the wind.

"You are a combatant. You fight the Peruvian army, correct?"

"Yes."

"But you like to hit women?"

He closed his eyes.

I walked over to the man with the wounded shoulder. I put a bullet in each of his kneecaps. The sounds startled his comrades. The scream echoed, full of misery. Jair spat out a stream of brown juice, disturbed by the noise.

Returning to the two remaining Senderistas, I squatted down to speak at their level.

"One of you talks. One of you dies. I'm not going to kill both of you. No matter what, I am taking one of you back to Lima with me. It is up to that person if he wants to be tortured or not."

Ramfis bent over. "We're not fucking cops from your hometown. We're not going to slap you around and burn you. We're going to do things to you that you can't even imagine."

"When your mothers see your bodies," Jair added, "they won't even recognize you."

I still couldn't see the fear registering. These two were really gone, really brainwashed. Loyal soldiers—Guzmán was alive because of boys like these. Had they been university students? Or just street kids? They wouldn't have any documents on them. Everything would have to be extracted by force.

"Who's going to talk?"

The man who had struck the mother spat at me. I felt the saliva hit my cheek. It was thick. The spit of a dehydrated man. I took out a handkerchief and wiped it away.

"Open your mouth."

He didn't flinch.

"Open your mouth."

"You are an enemy of the people and you will die like the dogs who betrayed Mao."

Ramfis burst out laughing. Jair cracked a smile.

I stood up and signaled to them. "Open his mouth."

Ramfis and Jair kicked him over. Jair grabbed the rifle from the ground and beat the terruco over the head. When he was almost unconscious, they sat on his chest. Careful to avoid his teeth, they squeezed his cheeks and pulled at his chin. A small "o" opened up.

I made the other man lie on his face. I handcuffed his hands behind his back. Walking over to my men, I readied the gun.

I shoved the pistol past his front teeth, scraping them out of the gums. I pressed the rectangular muzzle down, deep into his gullet. His arms and legs thrashed madly, his breathing accelerated. The choking, sputtering sounds rose. They began to die away as I could feel the metal slide down his muscles.

I lifted my head to check on the passengers. All of them had their faces pressed to the windows, struggling to catch a glimpse of what was happening in the darkness.

Nobody wanted to see, and yet, no one looked away.

I found out that she already had a literature degree, but she was still studying for fun. She took classes at the Catholic University in anthropology, sociology, Quechua, history. Graduate seminars and introductory courses. It was a way for her to pass the time, a way to expand the mind without committing to anything.

We had no agents at the Catholic University. It was a private institution for high-achieving students—not all of them were rich, but the vast majority came from good families. There was no terrorist infiltration, security was tight, and everyone took their studies seriously. The professors were part of the democratic left; hardly any were affiliated with People's Aid.

Still, I needed an excuse to see her. I had to learn her routine. I had to learn everything about her.

A junior agent would keep an eye on her when I was busy, which was most of the time. He didn't question my orders. We wrote nothing down in those days. Everything was said face to face.

"Don't touch her, don't touch anyone she knows. You make no contact. Just keep track of her movements. Who she sees, what she does."

I didn't want to wonder about her anymore. I didn't just want to see. I wanted to understand.

She was a happy face in a crowd of serious young people. She liked to learn without trying to be an intellectual. She wore ponchos and coats and scarves over her dresses, draping herself in alpaca, protecting her soft body from the cold. Her nose would wrinkle when she was confused. Her teeth would stick out like a rabbit's when someone gave her kindness. She had a few friends, but she usually liked to sit alone, away from the vicious debates and gossip.

She was always sipping on something. On campus, she would buy a coffee. In the street, she would buy a fresh juice or a bottle of Inca Kola from a stand. She never seemed to drink water.

Her parents were quiet people. Dentists. They had a practice together. They left the house together, they returned together. They called their only child every day, gave her pocket money, insisted that she sleep over on weekends. Her mother was white, her father mestizo. They looked dull compared to her, just like everyone else. Indoorsy people, small people, colored gray from the white lights in their office. They worried a lot, always checking the garage door in their suburban house, always installing new locks and electrical wires. Slat steel fences. An alarm system. Barricading themselves in, preparing for the day when we couldn't keep them safe, when the terrucos would come down from the mountains.

The father made calls to Colombia—foreign dentists and doctors had the right to practice there, but they decided against moving. Bogotá had a surplus of dentists, there was no money to be made. They put the house up for sale, found no buyers and took it off the market. Careful people.

I liked that their daughter was so different from them. She gave coins and packs of cookies to street children and elderly beggars. She chatted with the taxi driver, with her neighbor in class, with the doorman at her lover's building. She was open and naive and easily delighted. She was a streak of light and pleasure in my gray city.

When I was a young man, I dreamed of young love. It did not

appear, not when I was a boy or an adolescent, not when I was a student or a cadet. How lucky I was to find her.

—

The highlands

In what is still known as the Emergency Zone, the emergency is over. There is no need for me to be here. But the state has learned its lesson. Every part of the territory must be manned. Every inch of soil must be watched over. So, here I am.

The village school only teaches the essentials. If the students want to pursue their education after age fourteen, they have to commute to the nearest town. The regional government has given me the authority to teach civics—a required course to enter high school.

I give lessons twice a week. Spanish is their second language. My Quechua is too weak to teach a curriculum. I just make an effort to speak slowly and clearly, like how El Chino speaks when I hear him on the radio. He hasn't changed.

The Agrarian University, where I first met him, took up a thousand acres alongside a road that led out of Lima. The mountains were close by, but they didn't obscure the few crucial hours of sunlight.

Ramfis and I arrived in the district of La Molina an hour before our meeting. Some guards and students watched us—everyone was dressed in comfortable work clothes. We stood out in our suits.

I remembered what the Doctor had told me about the rector the day before. "Go see the Chinaman at his university. He's interesting. Wants to get into politics."

All the buildings on campus were simple bungalows, plain buildings without glass in the windows. The walls were made of brick and sandstone, nestled between sprawling experimental farms and dairies. There were no shortages here: every few hundred feet, you came across some students selling milk, watermelons, empanadas, freshly squeezed papaya juice. Locals from the area wandered onto the campus, leaving their identity cards at the gate, to buy from the student farmers.

Ramfis scoffed. "Is it a university, or a fucking farmers' market?"

"They're making money. The university must get a cut. No other state school can say that."

There was no graffiti anywhere; the buildings and trees were untouched. Dogs walked about without a fear in the world, barking at the cows and horses. It was still early in the morning, but students were already huddled around professors in the fields, clipboards in hand. Bleating came from the veterinary building, mixed with the voices of trainees. We had to step aside for some tractors that chugged along, operated by nervous-looking young men.

The land never seemed to end. The flat acres were a rich, dark green, making for an oasis at the edge of a dusty road. Dry brown patches around the student pavilion acted as reminders of the desert, but no wrappers could be seen in the dirt. The backwardness of the countryside was far away from here, and so was the grime and noise of Lima.

The rector's office was in one of the bungalows, beside an arbor. His secretary offered us seats. From what I had seen, even in the poorest universities in the interior, rectors usually had lavish offices. This one was sparse—the chairs were wooden and simple. The walls were free of paintings. A floor heater was plugged into an outlet.

I heard the clink of a phone. A door opened. The rector emerged at precisely the time we were scheduled to meet. He was an Oriental, with tanned skin and deep lines on his face. He wore cotton pants, boots and a white dress shirt.

El Chino was taller than most Asians in Peru. His sleeves were rolled up—his arms were wiry, tough. A thin man, but formidable, with excellent posture. His small mouth broke into a big smile. His eyes crinkled under his oversized wire glasses.

"Good morning, gentlemen. Would you like some tea?"

We sat in front of his desk. There was a statue of Buddha in the corner of the room. Some embroidery clung to the walls. His window overlooked a traditional Japanese garden. There was a little pond, a path of smooth stones. So, he wasn't a Chinese; he was of Japanese descent.

He poured us green tea into small black cups. The steam rose, fogging up his glasses. Ramfis made a face as he sipped.

Seeing that I was eager to listen, El Chino skipped the pleasantries and began telling us about his life. I had already read his file, but I still wanted to hear him out.

He spoke in clear, formal Spanish, without a Peruvian accent. He used no common expressions, no local jargon. He had been born in Lima, but you could tell that he had grown up speaking Japanese at home.

He had a halting, precise way of speaking, avoiding the use of any unnecessary words. Unlike most of the rectors I had interviewed, El Chino was not in love with the sound of his own voice, nor did he brag about his academic achievements. He simply told us that he was an agricultural engineer, and that his occasional lecturing at the Agrarian University had eventually resulted in his appointment to the rectorship. This humility was hiding the longer story.

El Chino had gotten a doctorate in agricultural engineering from the university he now presided over. But he had also studied physics and mathematics abroad, in Wisconsin and Paris. He hosted an early-morning show on state radio, where he discussed crop yields, farming techniques, and new regulations in the agricultural sector. One year earlier, he had been elected president of the National Association of University Rectors. He didn't mention any of these things to us. Either he was truly humble or he already knew that we had access to his dossier.

"My father was a tailor—but in Japan, he was a fisherman. I am also a person of nature."

He finished his tea and stood up.

"Let me show you around the grounds. I hope you both know how to ride a bike?"

He marched out the door. Ramfis looked shocked. I liked this Chinaman.

Outside, El Chino hopped onto an old ten-speed bike. The green paint was peeling and the pedals looked flimsy, but he mounted it with confidence. There were some other bikes leaning against the wall of his bungalow.

"My shoes," Ramfis muttered. I looked down at his shiny leather dress shoes and burst out laughing. Such a tough guy, and worried about getting mud on his feet.

"You stay here. We'll be back soon." I've never had a problem with a little dirt.

I got on a blue bicycle. It was a bit small for me, but it looked new and had thick wheels. I stabilized myself and pushed off, following El Chino. I felt shaky—it had been years since I had ridden a bike—but he was steady, the bicycle was a part of him, an extension of his wiry body.

We pedaled along a dirt path, cutting through the fields. The smell of manure was strong on this side of campus. It hung in the damp air.

El Chino slowed down so that we could ride beside each other. Students and teachers waved at him, shouting greetings.

He would steer with one hand and wave back, giving them his earnest smile.

"You're popular."

"I tell my colleagues in the association that they need to bridge the distance between themselves and their faculty and students. Otherwise, we can't build a sense of community."

He braked beside some workmen who were digging a trench. I braked as well. He chatted with them, asking about the pipes. They responded cheerfully, satisfied with the materials they had been given to work with. El Chino nodded briskly and wished them luck. Off we went again.

"We have our own sewage system—we need to make sure that the aqueducts aren't contaminated. Our irrigation depends on clean water. The municipality won't do it, so we hire the workers ourselves."

I clutched the handles as I went over a thick mound of dirt. "What are your thoughts about the economic situation?"

El Chino didn't answer for a bit. He was staring straight ahead, looking for the road where we had to make a turn.

"We need to get back to basics," he said. "The land is very rich. We have limited arable land, but the soil is the richest in the Americas. The agrarian reform devastated the country in the seventies—we are still recovering from that. But we have the engineers here, we are training hundreds of young specialists. There is no reason we cannot increase productivity . . ."

"But?"

He turned smoothly into a bend. I almost toppled over, but I recovered. We were heading for a massive garden covered in plastic sheets.

"You know better than I do that the security situation is getting out of hand. There's no use having agricultural engineers in Lima if they can't even go into the countryside safely. If Sendero catches them teaching the peasants or transporting machinery, they'll be killed. We've lost several alumni in the last decade. The south of Peru is not safe anymore."

"You've traveled around the country. You've advised the farmers, the ministry of agriculture. What's the solution?"

"I'm not a security expert." He braked outside the garden and swung his leg over the seat, popping down the kickstand with his boot. I did the same, happy to be back on my feet.

"No. You're just an engineer, a physicist, a mathematician, an academic . . ."

He smiled. His eyes squinted, looking happy and energetic.

"Sendero has very few members. The soldiers could crush them in a head-to-head battle. Why haven't they?"

"Because Sendero hides. They're in the villages. We can't tell who's a peasant and who's a terrorist."

"Precisely. However, we know for a fact that the vast majority of the peasants hate Sendero. If they didn't, we would have lost control of the country years ago."

"True."

"Instead of sending soldiers from the coast to the mountains to do the killing, the villagers must be given the resources to help themselves. They must be given training and weapons to defend their villages, to defend their land."

"The government thinks that would lead to lynching," I reminded him. "Anarchy in the countryside."

"There's already anarchy."

El Chino led me into an orchard. He nodded at some students working with spades. They greeted him warmly. He plucked two green tangerines from a branch and handed one to me.

"The government has failed in the war against terrorism. If they had spent the last few years working with the peasants instead of slaughtering them, Sendero wouldn't be such a threat. It's good to eat them when they're green, less sugar, more nutrients."

We peeled our tangerines. I kept the peels in my hand until I saw El Chino throw his at the foot of a tree. I did the same.

"Natural fertilizer."

"How have you taken care of the security situation on campus? Most of the public universities are out of control."

"We have an advantage here. The students are more serious—the entrance test is very difficult, very scientific and mathematical. There is no time for politics. We provide a lot of scholarships, a lot of free produce to people in the area . . . there's a kind of loyalty. More than anything, though, we have lots of security guards. The minister of interior knows that if he doesn't protect the campus, the country will starve. All of the agronomists and veterinarians come from the Agrarian University—our alumni manage all of the farm holdings around Lima."

"You know the minister of interior?"

"We meet once a month to discuss food security and the situation in the country's public universities."

"Powerful contact."

El Chino finished his tangerine, delicately licking the juice from his fingertips. "I have a feeling that you're even more powerful."

We got back on the bikes and rode past cactus plants and bright purple flowers. The campus had its own wells, giving a picturesque image to what was supposed to be a stoic technical university. There was no sense of strict order in the construction—everything was built using minimal space, working around the whims of the land. The students here were happy, meaty, browned to a crisp from all the outdoor work. The economic crisis and the terrorism had no home here—El Chino was administering his own village in a megacity. For how long could he preserve this utopia?

"You're interested in politics."

"I am."

"The Doctor thinks that you have a lot of potential. I do as well."

"Thank you."

"Tell me what you have in mind. Congress? Senate? The municipal elections are coming up . . ."

"Oh, I wouldn't want to waste your time with such small things." I braked. He did as well. There was nobody around except for some grazing horses. The trail was deserted.

"You want to run for president?"

El Chino smiled. "I'm not ashamed to admit that I like power. The only position worth having in this country right now is the presidency. If we don't get a competent executive soon, who knows what will happen?"

I began to answer him. He cut me off.

"I'm not saying that it will be easy for me to win. I'm just saying that, judging by what I see in the field, nobody would be able to govern the country as effectively as I could. Would you disagree?"

I thought about the elderly socialists and communists filing their congressional lists; about Vargas Llosa, recently returned from London, propped up by a fractured alliance of right-wing elites. The same old oligarchs were behind the scenes, writing the same wooden speeches that lasted for hours. None of the candidates inspired confidence. And none of them, as far as I could tell, were unbreakable.

El Chino continued pedaling. I followed him.

"I would need personal security. Some money."

Our budget was vast—what he was asking for wasn't exorbitant at all. And at that moment, there was no registered candidate who would have accepted our help—perhaps because we weren't the easiest men to work with.

"I'm not asking for charity. I'm asking for an investment . . . a partnership. I know better than anyone that nothing is free in this life."

"Maybe the Doctor wouldn't like that I'm asking you this . . . but I think that you're a decent person. I think that you should know exactly what you're getting into." He was crouched over his handlebars, looking ahead. He didn't look like the kind of man who did things spontaneously—he probably didn't need to hear what I was going to ask, but I decided to ask him anyways.

"Do you know who we are? I mean, do you *really* know?"

He parked his bike outside the rectory. I stayed on mine, watching him. He cleaned his glasses with his shirt as he looked straight at me, in a blur.

"I know very well who you are."

These stories aren't for the classes I teach. I cover a little bit of the republic's history, the different levels of government, the constitution. Democracy versus dictatorship. The kids find it pretty interesting, and they enjoy the trek up the hill to have class with me in the command post. I wear my formal uniform when I teach. It impresses them. They don't know that my rank of lieutenant is invented, or that I never fought in the war with Ecuador or won any of the medals I wear.

I make them take notes and I write up little tests—a woman in the village makes the copies for me. I note the grades in a folder and pass it on to their teacher. I don't think anyone looks at the grades. They just trust that all the kids will understand a little bit about Lima and the provincial capital, about the people who rule them.

I do have other duties. I march around the village with the reservists three times a month. Most of them are in their fifties— I keep them in shape, make them sweat a little. They do their jumping jacks and push-ups, run laps around the soccer field. I supervise them as they clean their old rifles. We check the contingency walls—mudslides are a big problem—and look around the village perimeter for any human tracks. Aside from our own, we've found none.

I have meetings with the mayor and the two village police officers. They give me a report on crime. Sometimes they ask me for help to bring a drunkard to the station—most of the calls they get are about a peasant beating up his wife.

Once, though, they asked me to take a guy to the provincial capital in the mayor's truck. I had to handcuff him to the passenger door. He was accused of raping his eight-year old daughter.

I had to control myself from killing that man, from throwing him out of the truck and running him over. I almost did it. I broke his nose as soon as we left the village. I slammed him against the dashboard. He didn't even protest. He just hunched over, blood gushing out of his nose.

"There's something about the highlanders," the Doctor used to tell me, when we traveled in the Andes. "There's something about the fathers . . . something a little sick."

The teaching, the training and the meetings only take up a few days each month. But the short bursts of socializing are draining. I give them all my energy. It makes it easier to return to the hill, to be alone.

I'm not supposed to teach the children about the terrorism. They're too young; the education ministry is worried that they'll be traumatized. But my students ask me questions, and I always answer them. I don't overcomplicate things; I don't give them any gory details. But I respect them and I answer them. They like that about me. The adults here don't talk very much. Parents are too scared to speak about the terror. It's a big mistake on their part.

"Did you fight in the war?"

"I did."

"All alone?"

"No, many of us fought."

"Was it the war against Chile? Or Brazil?"

"It wasn't against a country. It was against some very bad people, people from here."

"What did they want?"

"They wanted power. They wanted to control us. They wanted to destroy things and hurt people."

"Lots died."

"Yes."

"My dad died. My mother doesn't talk about him."

"I'm sorry. I'm very sorry about your father."

"It's ok. My brother says he's still with us. He's just gone away for a while. Dad takes care of us, he protects us."

"That's true. Your brother's very smart."

"How did you win the war? Did you have to kill the bad people?"

"We won the war because we worked together. We learned what the bad people were doing, and it became easier to defend ourselves against them."

"Was my dad brave?"

I knelt down to wipe the tears from her eyes. "I know he was."

"Is it hard? To be brave?"

"It is. But we have to try."

Some of the kids like to stay at the command post to do homework. I let them. I make them hot chocolate and try to help them with their other subjects.

There are moments when I feel that the parents are a bit afraid of me, afraid of what my uniform and my knowledge represent. But they have faith that I would never harm their children.

—

HER LOVER, THE WRITER, HAD A thin body, a pencil neck. He stood confidently, almost aggressively, usually with a frown on his face and sharpness in his eyes. While he had the skin color of a Spaniard, his birdlike features were those of a highlander.

He dressed like me. Dark hues. Black and gray. He was careful about the cold, though. Never stepped outside without a scarf in the mornings. She was a lot more carefree than her lover. He was worry, and she was freedom. He was hardened simplicity; she was soft elegance.

He had a small body of work: four or five short novels. Two collections of stories. A dozen long essays that were sold as cheap booklets. But, much like his physical body, it was surprisingly formidable; it had a presence that couldn't be denied.

He mostly wrote about his life, about mundane little experiences. The writing was simple, so simple that it gave you the illusion that anyone could do it. There were no magical occurrences, no fantastic events or lovable characters. Just stories, simple stories relaying things that had happened to him or around him.

The work was frugal—there was not one unnecessary word to be found in his bibliography. He trusted his readers; he didn't play games with them.

His father had wanted him to study at the Catholic University, but he opted for San Marcos—it was calm in those days, with a faculty full of novelists and poets. In the end, he never completed his studies: he worked on an uncle's plantation in Jauja and tutored private school students in Lima. He read a lot during this time, writing only on scraps of paper that he would quickly throw away. To become a real writer, he would have to go to Paris, to the city where the world's greatest writers had gone to write about their home countries. He needed to create a distance from Peru.

After some years of saving, he took an Air France flight on a tourist visa. He would end up living illegally in Paris for two years. He stayed in a rooming house and spent every penny he had to his name on bread, cheese, oranges, coffee and cheap bottles of wine. He wrote throughout the day and took long walks at night along the Seine.

The bohemian life didn't materialize. He wasn't interested in art; his French was weak, and he couldn't find the discipline to improve it. He found battered Spanish novels in the libraries, ordered the same things from the same vendors. He didn't speak with the Frenchmen in the rooming house. Sometimes he met other Latin Americans, but most of them were working in Paris—unlike him, they had money to spend. He couldn't afford the bistros they sat in; he couldn't afford the prices of wine in a restaurant. So, he stayed away from these gatherings, ate at home, worked on his stories. He could not be a García Márquez or a Vargas Llosa—he was younger, less talented, unknown, unimaginative, easily bored by his own work. He would make his way differently.

He could have moved to any city to live the life he had lived in Paris—he could have done the same thing in Lima. What he was really looking for was a place where he could be the stranger, where he could be truly alone. Not a soul knew him in Paris. He couldn't be part of the society. He could stay in his room and write and redraft, he could walk the streets like a shadow. He could eat to subsist, losing weight, yellowing his teeth, limiting the tastes of his stomach.

He returned from Paris at the end of the sixties, just in time for the military government.

The soldiers took everything—farmland, banks, factories, ports. His father lost the plantation. All he was left with was the big house in Lima.

His older brothers left the country to find work in Spain and the United States. He moved back into the family home.

His father sank into a deep depression. He passed the time visiting other destitute friends, drinking himself to death.

His brothers wrote to him from abroad. When he didn't answer them, they called him. They wanted their share. When they threatened to hire lawyers of their own, he assured them that as soon as the junta relinquished power, he would sell the house and divide up the shares. Until then, he would live in the house and write.

A few years went by, a few policies changed. He put the house up for sale, got a reasonable price, paid off the loan and sent his brothers their inheritance. He put his own share in a bank and rented a painter's studio in Barranco.

A collection of essays was published in Madrid. His first book sold in Lima. Another in Buenos Aires. The sales were underwhelming, but his publisher wanted more. He complied.

After more than a decade of obscurity, his work became popular. He converted half of the advances and royalties into dollars and put the money in an account outside the country. The rest of the dirty, colorful wads of Peruvian intis were stuffed in a box in the closet.

The more he made, the less and less he went out. He hired a woman to clean for him twice a week, buy his groceries, do his laundry. His money bought him more time alone, more silence. He walked along the ocean or went to a bookstore or a movie. But that was it. That was the small life he lived until he met her.

When I saw the openness of her face and the frustration of his, I could almost imagine his small pension. The months going by— the pages slowly churning out. The famished bite of bread after a day's work—the hunk of smelly cheese to end the meal, to silence the pangs of hunger. The crumbs on his floor, the stuffiness of his air. The stiffness of the body. The inability to exit the constraints of that body and be free. The shitting in the public lavatory. All of that was on his face. I could see it rip through his skin, I could see it mark his wrinkles and burden his nose.

Did he ever tell her about those days? Did she know what it was like to be afraid of not being who you wanted to be?

I would read his books, sometimes. They helped pass the time during stakeouts and flights.

I read about the peasants who moved into the landlord's aban- doned mansion. I read about a woman, traveling alone through the provinces. And about two former comrades, who, even after the war is over, don't know how to love.

Squinting at his words under the weak light, his paperbacks bouncing on my lap, I would recall having read them before. I must have borrowed his early works from the library at the Officers' Academy. After the drills, after diving to the bottom of the ocean or scaling the cliffs around Lima, I would lie down on my bunk and read, read for hours. I devoured everything to numb the pain in my bones, to stop the wandering in my mind.

"What are you doing, Captain?" Ramfis would call to me groggily.

"Nothing, brother. Just reading."

"Studying?"

"Mmm."

"At least you don't read the Bible. The last thing we need around here is a faggot on his knees, saying his prayers." I smiled at this, since I knew that Ramfis was actually quite fond of his junior cadets getting on their knees.

I heard him drag his feet to the corner. He unzipped his pants and began to piss in the communal bucket, groaning with pain.

"Reading won't save us out there, compadre."

"Neither will liquor. You already sound like an old man."

He laughed, shaking his flaccid cock in the darkness. "If I'm going to get shot at by Indians in the fucking mountains for the rest of my life, I'd rather be good and plastered."

Some of the other officers muttered for Ramfis to keep it down. He cursed them as he stumbled back to his cot.

"Always reading, compadre. How'd you end up here with us?"

Each time we returned from the provinces, we found that Lima was increasingly beginning to resemble a museum.

Dogs continued to appear, hanging from lampposts. Hammers and sickles were burned into the hills, a reminder that the terrucos were getting closer and closer. More and more electrical towers were bombed—the ruins were then draped in red flags, just in time for the TV cameras. Graffiti was a plague; slogans were daubed in red paint from the slums to the shopping malls.

Cars and trucks still honked, radios still played at full blast, but the human noise level was steadily declining. People scurried around quietly, doing what they had to do as fast as possible so they could get home before the curfew.

You ended up reading all day long. The letters were big, you couldn't miss them.

THE BOURGEOISIE WILL NOT ESCAPE THE POPULAR WAR
THE COUNTRYSIDE WILL COME TO THE CITY
THE PERUVIAN PEOPLE WILL CROSS THE RIVER OF BLOOD

The lines to enter the embassies went around the block. Nobody was being picky—Miami, Paris, Montreal, Toronto, Mexico City, Cochabamba, Sydney, Santiago, Newark, Paterson— it didn't matter, it was time to leave.

My own family left. My aunts and uncles, my cousins. They joined the one million who managed to get visas.

I could have left as well. I had enough money—they had begun to pay us in envelopes full of dollars because of the hyperinflation. The weight was dependent on our results. I could have also walked into an evidence room or a bank and helped myself, nobody would have touched me. Even if I didn't leave with much, I spoke English. I had studied some law. I could have started a life somewhere else. But, like many others, I didn't.

"Give me one good reason why you won't come with us."

"Because this is my home."

Whenever he was in a good mood, he would take her to Kennedy Park to have a cup of strawberries and cream. It was named after the American president who was shot. People had stood in the park and cried for him.

She liked to look at the cats—the park was full of them, the municipality encouraged them to keep the rat population down. There were also painters and jewelry makers selling their wares. Fire jugglers, clowns, popcorn vendors, tourists snapping pictures. He thought it was a tacky outing, but he made an effort.

She snacked on junk food—picarones and syrup, caramel popcorn, a candied apple. But the strawberries and cream made her really happy. It was a dessert from her childhood, when she had been even more carefree. It was nostalgia in a cup.

Whenever they sat in a bistro beside Kennedy Park, he drank pisco in a tall glass with lime and ice. He would smoke his Incas, the domestic cigarettes, the cigarettes smoked by the poor. They were black, rough, nationalistic. He would smoke one after the other, running his tongue over his stained teeth before taking a sip from the glass.

She didn't smoke—but whenever I saw them together, walking in the park, sitting in the back of a cab, I could tell that she liked the smell. She never bothered him about smoking; she would lean her head against his jacket when he exhaled.

They would sit by the park for hours, unhurried, savoring every drop and every breath.

I wanted to smell what they smelled. I wanted to taste what they tasted.

She was leaning over to stroke a white cat under the chin when a car bomb exploded. He threw her under the table in a second, wrapped his arms around her, pushed her into the ground. You couldn't hear anything, you couldn't see anything. It took a long time for my senses to adjust. My men were running, but I couldn't be sure. There were gunshots. The death toll would be high— couples, children, cats. Even if they weren't hit by metal or fire, the force of the blast would have thrown bodies around.

I poured water into my eyes, blinking until I could see again. My ears adjusted, the roaring was silenced. A woman, covered in dust and blood, wandered through the middle of the park screaming for her child.

She was playing with a cat. Where is she? *Where* is she?

Where is she? The question rang in my head as I lurched through the grass, trying to find the mother's daughter. And the mother was suddenly my mother, and she wouldn't stop screaming. The sound kept me in deafness as I searched for her daughter, who was suddenly my sister.

Whenever she had gotten lost, whenever she had wandered

away, I had always found her. I would feel my heart settle and I would see the colors return, and her hand would be in mine. She was small, fragile; it always seemed like she was about to slip away, about to leave us. And even after she really did, I still found myself reaching for her hand, for the colors.

A gardener caught the woman as she fainted. She went limp in his arms, the way my mother went limp in mine.

We reached the naval base at one in the morning.

The landing zone was right on the water. You could only see navy ships—fishermen weren't permitted to cross into these waters.

Only the air traffic controllers and I knew who was coming. None of the agents asked me; they understood the protocol.

The drivers kept the engines running. We leaned against the doors and smoked, rubbing our hands in the cold. There was no coffee.

Lima's lights illuminated the smoggy sky. The base had gone dark.

A buzz sounded. It was faint, but it slowly grew louder.

A hulking shape hovered over the rippling water, heading towards land. My hair was thrown around by the force generated from the blades. The helicopter had been darkened for security.

Naval officers on standby ran to open the doors. The deputy secretary jumped down with their help. No luggage. The officers formed a circle and hustled him to us. They pushed him into my car. I got in as soon as he was inside.

The doors slammed, the engine revved. We just missed the boots of the navy boys as we drove off the landing zone. The helicopter was already gone.

The convoy sped through the checkpoints—the guards knew not to stop us—and began speeding on the highway that led from

Callao to Lima. The curfew was in effect; there was no traffic on the unlit roads, just a few police cars and supply trucks.

Atkinson was tall and thin, dressed in a brown suit. His narrow face was puckered sourly under his white hair. His glasses were dislodged on his nose.

He didn't bother to make small talk. I had no orders to brief him, so I also kept quiet.

Atkinson stared intently out the tinted windows. He tried to take in the crammed, mismatched storefronts. At each intersection, he scanned the pavement and the tenements, stretching his long neck to catch a glimpse of the hills in the distance. He pressed his nose to the glass in an effort to see the shantytowns.

We were going at 100 miles an hour. I doubt he saw much. Still, he couldn't miss the filth, the greenish-black of the buildings, the teetering of the slums. When had he last been here? Had he been expecting red flags, Senderistas on the march?

In the daytime, he would have been able to see the graffiti and read the words. It was everywhere. At nighttime, it blended into the walls—the ugliness of Lima became one.

Atkinson didn't need to see anything. The precaution surrounding his arrival was enough to confirm the seriousness of the situation.

Out of the corner of my eye, I saw a dog hanging from a pole. I don't think he saw it.

We reached the city center. Homeless families and drug addicts were clustered under the statues in the middle of the roundabouts, marking plots on the raggedy grass. Sleepy eyes peeped at the convoy.

The driver's radio crackled. "Take a left at Angamos and circle back. Area not secure."

Atkinson listened—his Spanish was fluent—but didn't flinch.

He kept his eyes on our twists and turns. The churches and office buildings formed a narrow tunnel all around us.

We made a final turn, reaching the gate at the back of the Government Palace. The men from Special Forces were expecting us—they wore masks and carried flashlights and machine guns. Snipers on the roof gave them cover.

They threw open the gates as we pulled into the lot, slamming them behind us as soon as the last car entered. Then, they ran out through a small door into the streets, guns extended, prowling for any sleepwalker or junkie who may have spotted us.

"I thought we were going to the embassy?" Atkinson uttered his first words to me.

"The president felt it was more secure to meet you here. The road to the embassy is too exposed."

"The Ambassador will be present?"

"Yes."

"Good."

We got out of the car. The protection unit flanked us until we entered the palace. When we reached the first sitting room, a side door opened. We went down the stone steps until we reached the catacombs.

The smell of clay and trapped air hit us hard as we moved past the displays, ducking our heads to avoid hitting the rough ceiling. Lamps lit the way.

The church had used the tunnels during the Inquisition. Beneath our feet, hundreds of bodies, mangled by torture devices, were buried under mud and rock.

We reached the bunker. Two men in black uniforms and red berets guarded a steel door. They carried assault rifles. At this point, we had no choice but to hand over our identification cards and sidearms.

El Chino had ordered the bunker built in his first few weeks in office. He had five children, and a more cautious nature than his bohemian predecessor. Sendero frequently planted bombs near the Government Palace. In the days after his inauguration, terrucos made an assault on the front gate in broad daylight. All of them were killed, but never before had they tried something so brazen. A detachment of anti-assault troops was added to the security detail, and the catacombs were opened up.

The air in the bunker was fresh, pumped in by machines. The cleanest air you could find in Lima, bottled. Atkinson tidied his hair. His face was rosy from the heat of the car. He looked more comfortable in the bunker—he was a man accustomed to basements, artificial lighting, air-conditioning.

The bunker was a maze of corridors and rooms. There were couches covered in books, girls' clothing, action figures. The children were living down here. We arranged another convoy to take them to school every day. Someone had suggested that El Chino have them homeschooled. I laughed when I heard this—a Japanese would rather have dead children than children who skipped class.

The boardroom had a table where we could all sit on leather swivel chairs. At the head of the table, there was a whiteboard. This was where the strategy sessions were held.

The president and the Doctor walked in. The American ambassador trudged after them, groggy and red-eyed. We all stood up. El Chino shook hands with Atkinson. The other two did as well. We all sat down, except for Atkinson, who remained standing.

"Whenever you're ready, Mr. Secretary."

Atkinson strolled over to the whiteboard, grabbing a black marker. He was used to lecturing, he didn't have a trace of self-consciousness. He didn't mince words or slow down for anybody to catch up. His Spanish was irritating, but understandable.

"Argentina has provided military bases and empty farms along the border for the exclusive purpose of training. At the moment we have . . ."

He grabbed a pen to mark down numbers and nationalities:

5,000 Arg.
1,000 USA.
1,000 misc. (Col. Mex. Chile. Brzl.)

"Seven thousand troops."

"There can be more. We have a DEA force working out of Medellín that can be airlifted to provide technical support."

"What kind of equipment has been set aside for an intervention?"

"Submachine guns. M82s. LAV-25s. Air support is extensive."

"Who would provide the planes?"

"The Chileans."

The Doctor rubbed his hands together nervously. "Pinochet isn't in charge anymore . . ."

"No, but he's still in command of the military. They're willing to provide bombers."

"How fast can these men be airlifted?"

"In a matter of hours. They're reserved just for this mission; all of their training has been devoted to mock scenarios. The Shining Path doesn't have any planes or rocket launchers, so we have the advantage of entering the airspace without issue."

I watched Atkinson. He looked as determined as he had during the congressional hearings in Washington—he had devoted much of his career at the State Department to Peru's situation. Before that, he had studied Sendero's activities and written articles on terrorism. A hopeless man. With hopeless causes.

I watched El Chino as well. He looked perfectly calm, his chin resting on his hand, his glasses lowered.

"Mr. President," Atkinson said, after he had covered the board in lines and numbers, "I don't mean to suggest that these are the only options. We know that you have changed the direction of the war. We want to support you and hear what you need before considering the worst."

The American ambassador added to this. "We're just concerned about another Cambodia. Better to be safe than sorry."

The Doctor broke in. "This isn't a Khmer Rouge situation. Sendero doesn't have hundreds of thousands of fighters. They have a few thousand, maybe twenty thousand at most. The issue is that they aren't all in one place. There isn't a jungle we can bomb. The terrucos are everywhere, they hide in the population."

"That may be so, but in the case of a general collapse, there won't be any option other than traditional military action. The anti-subversive strategy has so far been—"

"A failure," El Chino finished the ambassador's sentence. "Yes. You're correct. And that's why we're doing things differently now."

"The last two governments refused to trust the people. They put all their trust in the military, the police . . . and other security forces. They failed. Under three different administrations, Sendero has grown stronger. We feel their presence in Lima now—they've driven us underground—but we are the first government to change the tide."

"Tell us what you need, Mr. President." Atkinson folded his hands behind his back. He was still standing, his head slightly bowed out of respect.

"I am going to close the Congress and the Supreme Court soon."

The ambassador's eyes widened. Atkinson nodded, as if he had already thought about this.

"For a short period of time," El Chino clarified. "Six months . . .

a year, at the most. It will allow my government to introduce some new emergency measures."

"What do those entail?" Atkinson sat down. He took out a pen and notebook from his suit jacket and bent over to write.

"The judges presiding over terrorism trials will be masked. They have a fear that their identities will be revealed—we need to assuage that fear. We will also be able to detain suspects for as long as necessary. Our soldiers and our police are demotivated, but they are loyal. There won't be any issue if we increase the prison population, they can handle it."

"SIN has already stepped up the effort to catch Guzmán. Interrogations are underway as we speak. With emergency rule, they'll be able to operate faster, disrupt the institutions that protect the terrorists."

The president poured himself a glass of water. His hands were steady. "The most important emergency measure will be the arming of the peasants."

The American ambassador looked aghast. "Mr. President . . . forgive me, but do you believe . . . is that really a sound course of action?" He looked pained as he asked this, not wanting to break diplomatic protocol. El Chino smiled at him benevolently.

"I understand your concern," he said, switching to his gravelly English. "The last two presidents were scared to arm the highlanders . . . even though the highlanders have been the principal casualties of the terrorism."

Many highlanders fought valiantly against the insurgency. Some of the Indians had been a tad overzealous, killing journalists who ventured too far into the Emergency Zone, mistaking them for terrucos.

"If we do not trust our own people, if we rely on our soldiers— or on foreign soldiers—we will lose this war. We will elevate the

Shining Path; we will make them look like underdogs fighting great powers. We need the Peruvian people to fight Peruvian terrorists."

Atkinson was still scribbling away. The Doctor watched him with a look of amusement.

The ambassador sighed. "So you don't see any alternative?"

"I have traveled throughout the South—I won all of the southern provinces in the election. The people are desperate. They need to be able to protect their villages and towns at night. They need to break the control that Sendero has over their land." He leaned back in his chair. "If we refuse to arm the peasants, we will lose half of the country within the next few years."

"The president is right." Atkinson put down his pen. "Sendero already effectively controls a third of Peruvian territory. It doesn't matter how many soldiers you send, there is too much ground to cover. A full-scale invasion of the countryside would be like another Vietnam. Guerrilla warfare at its worst."

The Ambassador turned to El Chino. "Is there a chance that the peasants would use the weapons on each other?"

The Doctor snorted. "My concern is that they'll join Sendero. We'll be giving them the weapons they need to win the war." The ambassador nodded emphatically, agreeing with this nightmare scenario.

"Anything is possible," the president stated. "There are no sure things in this country. But the peasants are suffering. They are desperate. If we train them, divide them into small self-defense committees and work with the elders, I am convinced that they will be effective."

I admired his bluntness. He had the capacity to separate himself emotionally, to look at things as they were. The attacks on his life had not made him lose his nerve.

El Chino looked at the Doctor. "They will, of course, still be under the supervision of the security forces."

"You just want to give them a bigger role in the war," Atkinson clarified for the ambassador's benefit. "Have them put some skin in the game."

The president smiled. "You could say that."

"I think that sounds very reasonable." Atkinson looked to his country's ambassador for agreement. He assented.

"Please tell us what you need to set these committees up, Mr. President."

The Doctor held up a hand. "I'm curious, Mr. Atkinson. You are a deputy secretary . . ."

"The deputy secretary of state . . ."

"For Latin America," the Doctor smirked.

"What's your point?" Atkinson snapped. He didn't like having to address the president's subordinates.

"In what way are you responsible for weapons procurement?"

"The administration listens to all my recommendations. I've been in DC for a long time."

I pulled out a document that I had been keeping folded up in my pocket since our last meeting with the high command. Atkinson began writing again. In addition to the main request of fifteen thousand new or lightly used rifles with adequate supplies of ammunition, I read out quantities and brands of binoculars, bulletproof vests, night vision equipment, two-way radios and several million dollars' worth of other gear that I judged the Americans either already had in their possession to lend us, or would be willing to buy for us. I worried that they would find the request to be outrageous, but neither Atkinson nor the ambassador batted an eye at my words. In their long careers, far more dollars and bullets had passed across their desks.

Atkinson wrote like a man possessed, and then read everything back to me. He got every word. The president confirmed my requests.

"I appreciate your solidarity with my country," El Chino praised Atkinson as they shook hands at the end of the meeting.

The deputy secretary beamed. "I've always loved Peru. I used to be in the Peace Corps," he said proudly. "I taught in Ayacucho."

His past was met by an uncomfortable silence. Ayacucho, now a bastion of terrorism, was no longer a welcome place for any of us. The idea that this bookish American had once taught there was almost laughable—it was an image from another time, another country.

He had spent the last decade of his life advocating for us. We were his pet project, his purpose in life. What would he do, if we somehow managed to stabilize ourselves?

Understanding that he had been too enthusiastic, he resumed a solemn look and said goodbye. We had to get him back to the naval base before traffic started—he would be a prime target for Sendero.

On the silent ride through the city, I watched Atkinson see Lima in the first specks of daylight. His face was blank, but I could tell that he was shaken to see the haggardness of the people. The immensity of the hills was palpable—an overcrowded mass lumbering over the graying buildings and rotting wood. Unlike in Mexico and Colombia, countries that he was also deeply invested in, nobody here looked capable of robbing a car or committing a murder. The people moved like ghosts, timid at the first sign of daylight. There was no strength or agility in their skinny, stooped bodies, but it did not mean that there was no hatred in their sullen faces. The Indians, in their flight from the countryside and their settlement in the capital, had learned to live with fear and hunger. They were strangers in their own country, visitors from another planet.

Atkinson watched their glassy black eyes as they boarded combis and walked across the roads. There was still an effort to keep clothes neat, faces clean, but the poverty was clear in every rip in the fabric and every patch on the skin.

The wind blew sand into their black hair—they lazily brushed at it with their fingers. Dust was part of their existence. It could never be washed away.

"The sky is so gray," he murmured, as he turned away from Lima. "But it never rains here, does it?"

"Never."

The French image of the presidency ceded to a Japanese one. There were no more parties, no more obstacle courses. Bribes were simplified, handed out in bags without any trappings or ceremony. Peru had to become more practical. Instead of aiming to be European, a vision better suited for a smaller, darker race had to prevail.

The businesspeople, the workers and the peasants were happy to tap into Asia. They received aid money, tractors and investors. However, not everyone was pleased with this shift in priorities. Diplomats were ordered to abandon the embassies in Paris and Brussels and move to Jakarta and Manila. Cultural attachés were sent to court American industrialists. The artists lamented the move towards technology. El Chino's program was too crude for the writers and poets—it was offensive, uncreative, standardized.

El Chino was a simple man. Ten gray suits. Tea and toast for breakfast. Fish soup for lunch. Green chicken and rice for dinner. No beef. No alcohol.

He would sleep for five or six hours at most. Pedal on his stationary bike and read his briefing papers.

Moving him around the Andes was difficult. He had to wear a bulletproof vest. He sucked on lozenges between stops to recover his voice.

We moved quickly. His speeches could not last more than ten minutes. None of us breathed as he walked through the crowds. We pressed around him tightly, but the Indians always managed to stick their hands through our barricade of flesh. They touched him and kissed him. They had never seen a president before.

It would have been faster to move around by plane, but the airports in the small cities weren't secure. If he wasn't in a helicopter with the air force, he was with us on the road. He didn't spend more than three or four consecutive days in the capital. He was determined to survey the countryside. He didn't want his authority compromised by Sendero.

When he wasn't in the capital or in the interior, he was taking the presidential jet to New York and Tokyo to woo investors and ask for aid. We would see him on television, speaking in his gentle English and Japanese, repeating his talking points.

Poverty does not necessarily mean violence. There is no need to be afraid of us.

We are removing the violent elements in our society.

All of our countries have been poor, at one point or another. We are not so different, you and I.

"It won't do you any good," the Doctor would complain to the president, as I strapped the vest around El Chino's chest. "They'll shoot you in the head. They'll blow you up."

"I need to see my people. I need them to see me."

—

The highlands

I take them to play soccer when class has gone well. They could play by themselves, but they like it when I join them. I use my participation as a reward.

We walk down the hill to the soccer field. It's a dirt field—the municipal field—but I have made sure that there is nothing sharp jutting out of the ground. The goalposts are new.

I'm not very good. They get a kick out of me missing a goal, or losing control of the ball. I do my best to pass, to stay out of the way.

They're excellent footballers. The girls play in the first half, but then they decide to sit on a bench and watch. It's a wise decision. As the game goes on, the boys seem to gain more energy. They become more aggressive, less chivalrous.

Someone falls down. Someone gets tripped. I stand between the insults and the flailing fists. I correct them without raising my voice. Their little bodies fly into a rage. It's as if I'm not there. They curse, they wound. There is no adult, no teacher, no lieutenant. I am invisible.

They watch the national games on their televisions. Some of the luckier ones have gone with their parents to see the provincial league games. They know the rules. This isn't a free-for-all scrimmage. It's a serious game, a battle. Every foul is called.

I'm not immune to the violence. The ball flies at my face, striking me. I get kicks to the shin, I stumble and fall. I put on a brave smile. When a lip splits open or a leg gets scraped, I assume the role of medic. I keep some bandages with me, a bottle of rubbing alcohol. I clean the wounds and try to soothe the sniffles and tears.

Sometimes I get frustrated. I'm too old for this. They should play by themselves, sort out their own disputes. But I realize that things are better when I get involved. The tensions die more quickly. The score is more even.

I get the ball. I aim at the net. The boys step aside—they are giving me a chance to score. I kick.

"Goal!"

They scream. The girls rush the field. The boys pile up on my shoulders, bringing me to the ground. Goal.

———

THE SELF-COUP. THE COUP FROM ABOVE.

The Congress, the Senate, the Supreme Court. Those were the highest-profile targets.

El Chino didn't touch the newspapers or the television stations. He gave orders to allow the journalists to wander around—so long as they didn't interfere with the work of the police or the army, they could proceed. The Doctor visited the most ethical publishers and producers with briefcases full of money. Peruvians cheered in the streets when the parliamentarians were dragged away in handcuffs.

All the action was downtown, but I had different targets in mind.

I sent Ramfis to the School of Lawyers. They grabbed the dean right outside the building. He was very handsome, with fluffy hair and pressed pants. His pink face turned awfully red.

"Where's the money?"

"There's no money here."

"Every lawyer in the country sends you a check every goddamn month. Where the fuck is the money?"

He refused to answer. A sergeant beat him over the head with a rifle. He put up a fight, he wasn't used to being questioned by law enforcement. There was a big scene; they finally arrested the dean, put him in a police van. Ramfis radioed me.

"They won't keep any cash on hand. It's probably all out of the country. Long gone. Just get whatever documents you can."

The lawyers were guarding information—they had their own language, their own system. They were not accountable to the country.

"It'll take years to go over all of this."

"What's the rush? We have all the time in the world."

At People's Aid, we kicked down the door. Everyone had to lie on the ground. We took identity cards, wallets. Compared them to our lists and photographs.

In the earlier raid, one of the lawyers had bitten Ramfis. But at People's Aid, nobody put up a fight.

We rounded up dozens of people and put them in a truck. Sent them to the SIN building.

"Put them in the basement. No phone calls. Don't register anybody."

They were crying. Most of them were students, but there were also some union representatives, an old professor from San Marcos. He kept playing with his glasses. Jair took them off his face and crushed them under his boot.

"I want every document in this building. Put them in the cars. I want the fucking copy paper, the newspapers, everything."

We found a safe. I put my gun against a young woman's head. She seemed to be the administrative type. She sobbed, she punched in the code.

American dollars. Checkbooks. Lists. Blueprints. Some gold bars and coins.

Jair sneered. "No intis? Fucking terrucos . . ."

"Don't log anything. Divide the money. Every man will get a share."

I could feel the pleasure of the men around me as I commanded this. They began screaming at the prisoners with more enthusiasm, they searched with more vigor, tearing up carpets and paintings with knives.

"I want names, I want numbers, I want addresses, I want family members."

They sliced their way into the couches, they put their ears to the staircases and the walls, tapping away. The women were frisked aggressively, they closed their eyes and screamed as their breasts and crotches were grabbed. Their fear was immediate now. They had trafficked in it for years, but it was always far away from them, something distant, something political. Now, it was here, in their house, right in front of them.

The pillars meant to support the electric train still stand along the highways. García got hundreds of millions of dollars in concrete kickbacks. The train was never installed.

Planted across Lima, the gray slabs are unusable, unmountable. El Chino decided not to pay for the train tracks or the train. There were more pressing expenses.

Millions of people pass by the pillars as they go to work each day. Hardly anyone bothers to look up and curse at the reminders of unkept promises.

The gray cement that had once matched the sky slowly took on the colors of brown and green. Stained from the soot in the air, from the sewage of the Rímac River that splashed on them whenever the water levels rose.

As the capital began to feel more and more like a ghost city, these pillars added to the sensation. They were tall, silent observers, watching over the people, blocking their path.

—

We operated better in the darkness. We never admitted that, but it was true.

Whenever Sendero took down the electrical towers, it gave us a kind of pleasure.

The light was our enemy. Darkness was our ally.

We could scoop people up as they walked home. We could do a raid and take the bodies with us. Limeños were too busy trying to find candles, trying to feel their way back to their families. Nobody saw us.

Everybody seemed to forget that the terrucos couldn't see either. They also preferred to operate in the darkness, but they didn't have the cars we had, the night vision goggles, the flash grenades, the helicopters. New equipment, courtesy of the Japanese and the Americans. Courtesy of El Chino.

You could hear curses from the hospitals. When the power went out, the machines wouldn't work. Nothing pumped the hearts. The surgeons turned on headlamps, bowed their heads, prayed for the generators to kick in.

Cars would hesitate through the streets, the drivers unstable. There were no lights to guide the way. You drove in tunnels of darkness. The rumbling of trucks came to a halt. At the unlit gas stations, the braver motorists kept pumping. The more intelligent ones, no longer able to see if anyone was approaching, locked themselves in their cars.

Soldiers ran through the streets near the Government Palace. Flashlights guided the way. Streaks of light touched the vacant faces in doorways.

The airport became a murmur of voices. None of the flights could take off, the control towers were dead. Pilots whispered to flight attendants. Old ladies sitting at their gates began to cry.

"Sendero is coming for us."

Their husbands comforted them, more concerned about how they would make their connections or get reimbursed by the airline.

Our helicopters took to the sky. They hovered over the airport, over the Government Palace, over the major highways—there would be no invasion, there would be no breach of the capital.

The police withdrew from the slums and the high neighborhoods. Stacks of uneven bricks towered over them as they sped down the hills. They hoped that the car batteries and headlights wouldn't die. They passed gangs of young boys awaiting the women caught outside during the blackouts.

Most of our time was spent walking up steps. Ten floors. Twenty floors. We had to secure the ministers, the top businesspeople. We caught some of the sympathizers in their penthouses—we surprised them, they thought that the broken elevators would discourage us.

The hammers and sickles would burn brightest on the night of a blackout. The terrucos scorched the hills, running over the sand and rock, dribbling gasoline over kindling. That was all you could see, the orange glare from the hills. It terrified the people, adding to the chaos on the roads.

For us, fire was warmth in the cold of endless night.

A doctor is very useful in times of war. A surgeon, even more so.

Sendero was infinitely grateful for the medical support it got from People's Aid. Even if the highlanders didn't believe it, the terruco boogeymen were human—voodoo and ritual killing didn't protect them from flesh wounds and disease.

Catching a Senderista medic was the equivalent of capturing a hundred fighters. The physicians talked easily—they knew locations and names. They knew which insurgent was sick, which one was long dead.

The interviews could last for hours. Torture was not necessary. We'd fill three or four notebooks during each session. Doctor-patient confidentiality disappeared in the basement of the SIN building. Ethics, like bones, are really very fragile.

The doctors and surgeons we interviewed were usually young graduates from the public medical schools. Some had been recruited and indoctrinated by Sendero, but a few of them entered medical school already armed with strong ideas about social justice. After getting their degrees, they moved to small towns in the provinces to do social work. In the highlands, they came into contact with the revolution.

When we had no more questions to ask, the physicians were subjected to a standard procedure. Ramfis called it "the autopsy of a broken man."

They were sedated to the point of a heart attack. Our amateur surgeon would then go to work.

The teeth and testicles were removed. Then, the fingertips and toes. Finally, the eyes had to go—the Indians say that if the eyes are gone, the dead man cannot accuse anyone of murder. We didn't believe that. But we hoped that the terrucos did.

The organs were harvested. The heart, the lungs, the spleen, the liver. The plasma. We gave the surgeons at the closest hospital enough notice—they saved a lot of people in the hours after interrogations.

After the body was sewn up, every bone was broken with a hammer. The thuds against the table resounded loudly in the basement. I had to fight the urge to tell the surgeon to quiet down. It was just my reaction—we could be as loud as we liked.

We never dumped the emptied bodies. We hung them from trees before dawn. We pinned cardboard to their chests and painted red letters:

WE WILL HEAL EVERY TERRORIST AND COLLABORATOR

It was our own performance art. Our answer to their hanging
dogs.

The people living in liberated territory had been forced to hand
over all of their currency. In President Gonzalo's Peru, everyone
had to live collectively, from the land. Cash was a mere tool in the
war against the military and the bourgeoisie.

The safe houses were full of money. Hundreds of millions of
intis, billions. The biggest cache was equivalent to a few hundred
American dollars.

The intis had first been issued in units of hundreds and thousands. Then, millions. Then, tens of millions. Even the terrucos
were not immune to inflation.

Half of the faces on the bills were unrecognizable. The treasury, ordered to print more money, had exhausted the supply of
famous Peruvians. Old statesmen were joined by generals who lost
the war with Chile. Then, in an act of social inclusion, Indian war-
riors who once rebelled against the Spanish were portrayed.

A stern poet. A smiling historian. Generals who never fought.
Descendants were surprised to see their grandfathers when the
grocer handed them their change.

The artists in the treasury still managed to make the brown,
blue, green, red and purple bills beautiful. Every few months, they
were given the opportunity to modify jawlines and invent new
crests. They found pleasure in their work, but their art would not
stand the test of time—each new release was followed by thousands
of previous creations discarded in the streets.

No matter how much effort was made to recreate notable
Peruvians, the faces on the bills still had an irritating quality. The

nineteenth-century scowls turned into sneers, mocking the people with their worthlessness.

Since it could barely buy food, the currency turned away from economics and found a new home in the cultural realm. Intis were glued together and framed, becoming political art. There was no money for construction paper in the schools, so teachers used the bills for origami projects. You could even write on the bills—the black ink stood out beautifully against the pale paper. The colors had bled and dulled, damaged by thousands of fingers and the rays of the sun.

—

The highlands

Someone is trying to take a tank of gasoline. I wake up to the sound. By the time I get outside, they are gone.

I smell sage in the air. The trees are swaying, I can hear the wind.

With my gun in one hand and my flashlight in the other, I survey the area. Two pairs of tracks. They weren't trying to set a fire—they had dragged the tank a few meters, they wanted to take it down the hill.

Maybe they wanted to sell it, but there's also the possibility that they wanted to smell it. Huffing gasoline fumes has become a common activity. The teenagers in the village have lost their taste for marijuana.

Some of the kids have died from the gasoline. Their younger siblings are still my students. Nobody talks about it. Not the adults, not the children. Whenever I bring it up to the mayor, he just sighs. "Such a shame. Such a shame."

I don't understand why they do it. They could be studying, playing soccer. Working on a farm. There's always extra work.

There's even television now—you can see satellite dishes mounted on the huts. That was unthinkable a decade ago. Before El Chino, there was hardly electricity in the provinces.

I think about giving some talks on drug and alcohol abuse. I have books on the subject—many of my men went through addiction during the war. Poor guys couldn't sleep unless they were drunk, couldn't wake up unless they got high. I implemented a "three strikes" rule. Some couldn't get themselves together, but I had success with a few.

Ramfis never saw the point of second chances—neither did the Doctor.

"Fucking junkies."

The mayor has already heard my proposal. He says it sounds good; he needs some time to consider it.

It's been a month since I made the offer. No response. I'm tempted to go to see him again, when the sun is up.

I should just start giving the lectures. Nobody would stop me. I'm sure I'd get a good turnout—so many families have been affected. If I keep asking, nothing will ever happen. Things are slower in the countryside.

I've become a cautious person. A person who asks permission.

I can't step on toes. The least powerful are the most sensitive, the most protective of their titles and jurisdictions and pensions. The mayor and his little policemen may seem insignificant, but even peons can cause trouble. They can sniff around your life, make guesses about your secrets. They can betray you, push you away.

It's best for me to stay within my role. Confine myself. The more needless exposure, the more I overstep, the more people see me, the harder it will be to stay here, alone.

I have always been invisible. That isn't hard. Being powerless is hard.

I shiver in the wind and go back inside the hut. The sheets are moist with my sweat. I change them and try to fall asleep again.

———

ONE WAY YOU CAN FIGHT DRUGS and alcohol is with food and sex.

After a good raid, I'd send the men to a whorehouse. For those who did not have wives or steady girlfriends, the visits were obligatory. They reduced the incidence of rape.

After we trained, or after everyone had fucked, we would go out for chifa. Eating Chinese food had a soothing effect—the food came out quickly, and there would be complete silence at the table while everyone ate.

No liquor or beer. Only Inca Kola. Liters of it. With ice, lots of ice. Peruvian Chinese food is too salty to go well with anything else. You need to sweeten and freeze your mouth between servings. You need to open your appetite so that you can eat more and more.

Chicken fried rice. General Tso. Honey fish. Ribs in rocoto sauce. Salt-and-pepper duckling. Thousand-year-old eggs. Fried won ton. Pork-and-shrimp dumplings. Beef and greens.

Sometimes they served us songbirds. You couldn't ask for them, the owner would send them to the table only if he was in the mood. They didn't have much taste, but the crunching of the little bones made for a nice sound. It added to the effect of the meal. To the ritual.

Chifa was our ritual. Our meal after a battle—or before a battle had begun.

There was no fixed budget. If the meal lasted five hours, that was how long it lasted. We only got up when every single man was satisfied.

We would arrive famished, but that wasn't a problem. Somehow, shortages never affected the Chinese restaurants. When El Chino sorted things out, the selection expanded even further. There were suddenly too many dishes.

They couldn't always be eaten.

The table shook. Nobody missed a beat; it was a tremor, maybe a bomb. Some of the light bulbs flickered, then went dark.

I threw some money on the table. We ran outside, down the street. The night sky was orange. Sirens screamed.

A car filled with dynamite had ripped through an apartment building. It was the worst we had seen. Fire was consuming the whole street. There was screaming coming from above. You couldn't see anything because of the smoke.

People carried little bloodied bodies. Fire trucks and ambulances drove onto the sidewalks. Survivors stumbled in our direction, stretching out their arms, clawing for support. Raw skin and exposed bone were covered in ash.

Alongside the neighbors and the paramedics, we spent the entire night digging through the rubble, trying to recover bodies. Our fingernails tore off; our hands were sliced and burned by the broken cement and hot iron bars.

The salt from the food coated my mouth. All I wanted was water.

She was always asking about his childhood. She was so fascinated by him. She wanted to understand why he was the way that he was. She wanted to recreate the younger version of her lover; she wanted to love him at every stage of his life.

I would listen to them at night. Usually, he would wave her questions away, too humble to talk about himself. But once in a while, he would surrender snippets of his past, about the boy he had once been.

He never had an appetite in his father's home.

He enjoyed visiting his grandparents. They let him eat slice after slice of bread, covered in butter and strawberry jam. He drank hot chocolate, without sugar or milk. He drank it like the adults, brewed in water with pisco.

He didn't want vegetables, a common thing in a child. But he also didn't like what his brothers loved. He couldn't stand fried chicken, couldn't bear the smell. He didn't like cakes—they were too creamy, they made him gag. He didn't like the American sodas or candy bars; they were too chewy, they left behind too much of an aftertaste.

His father worried about this. He ordered the maids to mix supplemental shakes and stuff ground beef into pieces of fried dough.

He balked at the smells and textures. Refused to eat.

He would sit on the chair, looking up at the ceiling, until the maids, realizing that this little boy was truly capable of starving himself, gave him some bread, some dry cookies. They disobeyed the master, they risked their jobs. It was no small thing.

She would coo sadly when he told her these stories. I could imagine her stroking his hair.

"Poor little boy."

The German girl was terrified. They sat her down in the chair behind the desk. Her eye shadow dripped down her cheeks, mixing with tears and mucus. Her red dress was torn. Her feet were bare.

The guys had been rough with her. They snatched her off the street, yanking her into the car as it was moving. I should have told them not to slap her around—there were marks around her neck, swelling on her forehead.

I watched her from the corner of the room. I hadn't eaten all day. The cigarette wasn't helping with my headache.

"Speak, you fucking Nazi. Why're you scared? Aren't you a brave little terruca?"

"You're a long way from Germany, little lady."

Her red hair and white skin made her stand out in the room. The rest of us had black hair and varying shades of brown skin.

I took another drag and thought about the "little lady." She wasn't really little—she was taller than all of us. And strong—her bare arms were toned.

Tough bodies, those Germans.

I wonder what made so many European anthropologists and sociologists buy plane tickets to Peru. They came to take classes, to teach us about our history. Staring at the mummies and the mountain women, they made up most of the tourism in the eighties. Some of them came to join the rebellion, backpacking around the Andes, whispering in the universities. They wanted to make contact with the Shining Path; they wanted to meet the legendary President Gonzalo.

Were their lives so empty in France and Germany that they had to come play guerrilla in Peru?

Most of them got bored before they found any Senderistas. Some of them were killed by the Senderistas before they had a chance to explain their intentions. But a few of them, like the German lady, made it far, they made it deeper into the organization than we had.

They kept screaming at her. Ramfis pulled out a blade, touched it to her shoulder. She was whimpering, apologizing in Spanish. I put the cigarette out into an ashtray and walked over. My men stood aside as I took the seat across from her.

"Do you understand why you are here?"

She didn't look at me, just looked down at the table and trembled.

"I'm going to speak in English so that we can have some privacy."

She looked up, surprised to hear the language she had learned before Spanish.

"I know Germans speak good English. Tell me if you know why you're here."

She shook her head. Ramfis slapped her. She yelped. I raised a hand, asking for calm.

"I don't know."

"Yes you do. You're on the Shining Path, my dear. That's not a good thing. If we were in the Emergency Zone, you'd be dealing with different gentlemen right now. But instead, you are here with me. Why don't you take advantage?"

She gave me a questioning look. I offered her my pack of cigarettes. I could tell that she wanted one; her fingernails and teeth were yellow, stained from nicotine. She shook her head.

I uncapped a bottle of water and brought it to her mouth. She leaned back and sipped a little. Her lips were cracked and bloodied.

"Does the embassy know that you're here?"

She nodded.

"But you've overstayed your tourist visa. And nobody at the German embassy has notified us . . . very strange."

"I'm not a terrorist."

"Nobody is accusing you of that. Believe me, I would know if you had done something violent. But you have come into contact with members of the Shining Path, yes? You have studied with them. You are in a Marxist study group. You bring them money."

She scrunched up her eyes. After entering and leaving Peru two times before, without issues, our conversation must have been very unpleasant, very unexpected. A blow to the ego.

"Tell me who you know in the Shining Path. Tell me who supports them from outside the country. You're a smart girl, you have a good memory. Help me do my job."

I couldn't picture the writer's lover in this situation. I couldn't see a girl like that ending up in the seat now occupied by this German bitch. Yes, she was happy-go-lucky, she was often unaware and trusting, but she wouldn't be attracted to violence or politics. She wouldn't find mystery and subversion so appealing.

"I have other people to visit. If you don't give me any information, I have to leave. I have to leave you with my men."

I waited a few seconds for my words to sink in. Then I sighed and stood up. She screamed. No. No. Don't go.

She gave me professors. Students. A woman who owned a hostel. Which hostel? Where is it? A meeting place. Where? Above a bookstore. Which one? How many of you?

The money came from a Marxist group in Munich. There were Germans who had links to some NGOs operating in the countryside. She even gave me the names of other foreigners in the country. Some Swedes, another German. Girls her age. She didn't care, she wanted to leave.

"Who is your lover?"

These foreign girls, they always took a lover. They couldn't close their legs.

She cried, pleaded with me. I watched her sob for a few minutes. Then I asked again.

She gave me his name.

I sent Jair and Ramfis away. "Go take a shower." I directed her to the bathroom. On the toilet seat, I left a pair of sweatpants and a sweatshirt.

She came out fully dressed, her face red from the hot water. I handed her a pair of sneakers, her wallet and her passport. I also gave her a document that would excuse her violation of visa conditions.

"My driver is going to take you to the airport so that you can buy a ticket and leave the country. I don't care where you go. But you leave today. You do not come back. Ever. Do you understand me?"

Yes.

She went into the airport without problems, without making a scene. People looked at her face. She ignored their stares.

She bought a ticket to Quito. She went to wait at the gate. She sat quietly. She had nothing to keep her hands busy, no books, no makeup. She waited for a long time—the flight was six hours away—until she finally got up from her seat and walked over to a stand near the gate.

She bought a magazine. And some chocolate. A glass bottle of Inca Kola.

After she ate some chocolate, she kept browsing. She bought a candy, Doña Pepa; the wrapper had a caricature of a cute black lady, hair made from multi-colored candies. She bought a keychain and a bottle opener. Some coca candies. Beads. A toy alpaca, made with real fur. She held it to her nose and smelled it.

I know that smell. I used to smell my alpaca slippers when I was little. It's like smelling a clean puppy, mixed with old, luxurious wood.

She put everything in a plastic bag and returned to her seat.

Behind the revolution, behind the ideals, there was a girl who wanted something sweet, a girl who was attached to the knick-knacks that our country produced. I could tell that she didn't buy them because she was hungry or because she had any real use for them. She placed them neatly in her plastic bag, maybe for later, maybe forever.

Sendero couldn't define her. Her radical friends couldn't hold her loyalty. Her secrets, her inner self, that was all she could hold on to. A smell, a taste, a feeling.

Our time together became one of her secrets. One of her memories.

The communist would pedal around the neighborhoods. He kept leaflets in his backpack. Whenever someone bothered to listen to him, he would stuff the pages into their hands, he would tell them about their role in society, about their responsibility to their fellow workers.

The people who stopped were usually nice. They nodded as he talked, waited patiently until he finished. They didn't scowl at his rat face. Some Peruvians are infinitely patient, putting up with anything.

It was almost tragic to see him in the basement. He was in shock. He stood against the wall with his back arched. He wasn't cowering; he had back problems. Probably from hunching over his handlebars for so many hours every day.

There was a sharp odor of mothballs when I got close to him. His sweater was old, covering up a shirt that must not have been washed in a long time.

The pamphleteer told me that she was the writer's student before she was his lover.

"I only knew him for a little while, when he was my teacher."

"That's a lie. He never taught classes."

The pamphleteer assured me that I was wrong.

"He did, he did. At the Catholic University. For a semester. I swear."

The famous writer was offered a full-time post at the Catholic University. His acquaintances were jealous, but to their shock, he turned it down. His advances and royalties gave him enough to live on, and he didn't get energy from being with people. To him, teaching was a waste of time. Everything he had learned, he had learned from books. He didn't want a job like that, a job where you had to go somewhere, answer to someone.

The following year, at the university's insistence, and at the prodding of his publisher, he eventually accepted a part-time lectureship, just to see what it would be like to teach young readers.

From the first day of the seminar, he became obsessed with her. Everything was written for her. He destroyed the writing of other students in front of the class. He paid no attention to the other girls; he emasculated the boys in front of her.

He stopped assigning work. He would mostly read aloud from books. He didn't want to have discussions. He didn't think that any of them—except for her—had anything worthy to say about the books he loved. He was protective of the authors that moved him. And he was protective of her, he only wanted her to speak. He didn't want anyone to criticize what she said.

It was hard to imagine love on his face. But I could imagine pain. Whenever he spotted her carrying a paperback that wasn't his own. Whenever she nodded at the comment of another, laughed at a classmate, touched a younger man's arm.

Despair.

He felt despair. And after years of living like a monk, he felt unbearable desire. He couldn't stand being watched, being listened to. He just wanted her. What was the point of being there? She was the point. It was clear.

She occupied the small life he had built. He needed to hear her voice; he needed her big brown eyes to remain focused on his motions. He needed to possess her body's curves, her gentle heart. Her existence made it impossible for him to go on being himself.

In a way, she destroyed him.

He left his teaching duties just a few days before the end of the semester. She abandoned her studies as well, for a little while. They devoured each other, after months of anticipation.

An empty office. A small bedroom. Two naked bodies. Unwashed sheets.

"You don't look like the type to study at the Catholic University."

The pamphleteer looked down at himself.

"We make our choices in life. I have taken a vow of poverty. To be closer to the poor."

He said this so innocently. He believed so deeply. A middle-class boy, playing the role of a poor man. It made me want to laugh. Or cry.

"Did you also want her?"

He twitched. Of course he had. We all had.

She was grateful. Grateful that he loved her. That was all it took.

She read his stories, she knew who he was, but none of it moved her. She didn't carry his books everywhere and sign up for the classes that taught them.

She was simply happy that she made him happy.

It took my entire self to contemplate the charitable act of giving yourself to the person who loves you.

What a generous woman.

———

The highlands

A man arrived in the village today. The children tell me about him.

"He has big glasses. And a small box, like a radio. But it doesn't play music."

I see him when I go to pick up some water bottles. He's walking around, asking questions. Not too many questions, just a few. Mostly, he spends time listening to the elderly villagers with an earnest expression on his young face.

I don't ask any questions about him. That would draw attention. And I know that no adult will give me any information.

The highlanders usually aren't fond of chitchatting with outsiders, but they are willing to answer him. Maybe they feel comfortable talking to someone who looks like them. The young man must come from Lima, but he has the copper color of an Indian. He has the flat black hair, the soft, high-pitched voice. Sad eyes.

The Indians are all about suffering. He immerses himself in their silence.

The Commission has extended its reach into the countryside. What was once an Emergency Zone is now accessible to scholars and researchers. They can take tours, rent rooms, hike the hills. The food is cheap and good, the air is fresh. Fieldwork is an excuse to take a vacation.

El Chino predicted that the Commission's activities would take place within a fixed period of time. There would be a big report, some publicity for a few victims. The opening of a museum. And then, things would return to normal.

It pains me to say it, but El Chino was wrong. He underestimated how lazy a culture can be, how much we enjoy repetition. The civil war is just too easy to study, too easy to write about and put on screen. Most of the country lived it—reporters and film directors don't struggle to recreate it or demonstrate its relevance. The Emergency Period is compelling—it gives Peru a dangerous allure.

The researcher never comes to visit me. He never makes his way up the hill. He has no interest in speaking to the authorities that protect him. He is satisfied with the old Indians who hang around the square playing dominoes. He practices his broken Quechua, chews coca leaves while he squats down beside them.

He is in the most creative period of his life, the most flexible period. He can live on bread and tea, he can sleep on the floor. He can fill ten notebooks and transcribe hundreds of hours of recordings. When he finishes his duties for his NGO or university, he will have enough material to write an essay, maybe a book. The literature of testimony sells very well. Until he has a family, until he has real responsibilities, the village will become his second home. The Andes will give him a chance to reflect and be inspired, if only for these crucial years.

If he sniffed around like a good investigator should, if he found out who I was, I think he would climb up my hill to speak to me. I have a lot to say. A lot of stories to tell.

———

WHEN SENDERO MOVED FROM the countryside into the city, there was panic. Especially among the upper class. Apathy turned to fear, and fear soon turned into paranoia.

There was the fear that the police were involved. It was an inside job, a conspiracy to help the violence spread. When the policemen became the primary victims of the terrucos, the paranoia shifted from them to the servants. The chauffeurs. The cooks. The gardeners. The maids. What did they think about the terrorism? Where did they live?

We also fell into paranoia. But it was impossible to surveil every domestic employee. We had to limit our investigations to those who worked for the most powerful businesspeople and politicians, the people whose demise could accelerate the collapse of the country.

in the hotel and the convention hall. He wanted to be alone to go over his notes.

She was mad at him for a couple of days. He promised that he would take her on a trip for New Year's. She forgave him. She came over, and they made love.

I watched him from behind the glass as he waited in line at customs. He carried two leather bags; he didn't check anything in. It was early in the morning. His hair was combed; he wore a dark suit and a bleached white shirt. She had made him send the clothes to the dry cleaner.

His eyes were exhausted. He had packed several books, but I could tell that he wouldn't read any of them. He would sleep on the plane. He would sleep in the hotel between his appearances. The trip would be a tired blur. The bags under his eyes wouldn't catch a hint of tan. He was meant for Peru's winters—he had no desire to see America's sun.

Have a good trip, my friend.

———

The highlands

"Teacher, how do you vote?"

"You pick the candidate you support."

"Yes, but *how*?"

"You look at the ballot—the sheet of paper. And you put an 'x' in the empty square beside the person's name and picture."

"And then?"

"You fold the paper and put it in the big white box."

"Do you write your name on the paper?"

"No. Your vote is anonymous."

"A-no-ny-mous."

"Yes. It's a secret."

"So how do they know you voted? How do they know not to find you?"

"Fine you. Charge you money."

"How do they know not to *fine* you?"

"You have to show your identification card. You have to sign your name on the registration. And the election officer makes you put your right index finger in blue ink. They take your fingerprint."

She picks up a marker and rubs it on the skin of her finger. "Like this?"

"Like that."

"Who are you going to vote for?"

"I can't vote. I'm in the army. Soldiers aren't allowed to vote."

She considers my evasive answer, drawing blue lines in her notebook.

"But when you are old, you can vote again."

"That's true. When I retire."

"When do you retire?"

"Like you said, when I'm old."

"Will you be sad?"

"I don't know. Maybe."

She turns in her chair to meet my eyes. She touches the top of her cheek and slides her little finger down the rosy skin, imitating a tear. I laugh. She laughs as well.

———

SHE STAYED IN HIS APARTMENT by herself. It would have been safer to go to her parents' house, but she decided to take advantage of his absence.

She seemed comfortable without him. She slept in. She watched soap operas, listened to music. Sang in the kitchen while cooking. Finished a book I had seen her carrying for months. Called some girlfriends on the phone, mused about making plans.

When he called her, she twirled the cord around her finger, slightly impatient. She was happy to hear his voice, but also looking forward to the meal she had left cooling on the table. It was a habit of hers to indulge when he wasn't around.

He was worried about her. Had she left the house? Had there been any blackouts? Why wasn't she staying with her parents?

Her voice was tender; it quickly soothed all of his anxiety. She didn't mention that she had organized his desk or cleaned out his closet; she knew he wouldn't want to start a fight when he returned. She took advantage of his absence.

"I miss you."

"I miss you too."

"I love you."

"How much?"

He laughed. "To the moon and back."

The flight was delayed, as usual. Peru was not a priority for the airlines.

I stood behind the glass. The customs officers worked diligently, stamping papers, pretending to keep busy.

I watched the passengers. None of them looked particularly happy to have arrived. Some were well-dressed, their suitcases overloaded from pleasure trips. Others had the lined skin and rough hands that come from cleaning up construction sites and scrubbing toilets.

Before, travel was only accessible to a handful of Peruvians. By the early nineties, it had been democratized—laborers, students and rich housewives stood in line together. A million Peruvians had fled. Millions more had plans to escape.

I remember predicting how the airport was going to change. When Guzmán was captured, when El Chino had finished charming the world, Peru was going to be a top destination. The expats would return. The tourists and miners would invade. There would be no more stealing from suitcases—everything would be formalized.

Late at night, his flight landed. I counted each second that went by between his seat in first class to the line at customs.

He was quick. First one out of the plane. The line had thinned; there were no international arrivals scheduled for a few hours. I saw him looking down at the officer, handing over his passport.

I pointed. "That's him."

An officer left my side and went out the door. They conferred. The passport was not handed back.

I could read lips from behind the glass. "Please come with us."

I watched to see how he would react. He didn't protest, but he was suspicious. He didn't have a bag checked in. He was Peruvian. This didn't make sense.

They sat him in a small room. I watched him from behind the glass. He slumped in the plastic chair, the two leather bags on the floor by his side. He crossed his arms, deep in thought. His hair was flattened, his face was greasy. There was a small white saliva stain on the edge of his lip. He had slept and drooled throughout his flight.

She would have been upset, seeing him like that. She would have cleaned his face with a hot towel, fidgeted with his hair. Brushed the lint from his jacket.

The guards wouldn't give him a straight answer. They left him in the room and locked the door. Only I could see him.

I drank a cup of coffee and smoked a cigarette. Watched him scowl, watched him tap his foot.

I went inside, closing the door behind me. Sat in the plastic chair across from him. Avoided his eyes, opened a file.

"How was your trip, sir?"

"Why am I here?" He ignored my question. His eyes were trained on me. He put his tiredness aside.

"We just have a few questions for you. How was your trip?"

I looked up at him as I repeated my question. He observed me, weighing his response.

He grunted. "Fine."

"Good. Good. I'm glad to hear that."

I flipped through the file, pretending to read the pages.

"Meet anybody you know in Florida?"

"The Peruvian consul to Miami attended the event where I spoke." He said this quickly. It was a kind of threat. Look who I know. See who I am. Don't fuck with me.

"Meet anybody from People's Aid?"

He blinked, completely caught off guard.

"What are you talking about?"

"Answer the question, please."

"You fucking . . . who are you?"

"You need to calm down . . ."

"No! No, fuck you!" he stood up in his seat and walked over to the mirror. He pounded on it. "Let me out! Now! Let me out!"

I didn't stand up. I didn't want to frighten him.

"I have nothing to do with any of those people. I won't be accused of this shit. I'm not talking to you anymore." He snarled at me, cornered and defensive. The veins in his neck pulsed; the force in his hand was strong. He shook the mirror as he slammed it.

I closed the file. The facade was unnecessary. Nobody was watching us. Nobody could hear us.

"It must have been a treat for them to meet you."

He turned and stared at me. His mouth was open. He was panting, breathless from his rage. Locks of black hair fell across his forehead.

"Readers rarely get a chance to know the authors they love."

He turned away from me and walked over to the door. He jiggled the handle. Slapped the frame. His face was red. He was fighting the urge to attack me.

"For me to see you now, to be here with you, it's an honor."

His eyes welled up. He sensed that something was very wrong. He feared the worst.

"I have nothing to do with any terrorists or any criminals."

"I know. I know."

"Let me go. Please. Let me go."

We got Guzmán. He was living on the second floor of a house in Chacarilla. The rich woman giving him refuge was the owner of a dance school. If she had groveled, we probably would have let her go. Instead, she raised her fist and screamed like a madwoman, announcing her willingness to die for President Gonzalo. We paraded her for the press. She got twenty-five years.

I wanted Guzmán executed. The Doctor didn't have a preference between a death sentence or a life sentence. It was in the president's hands.

El Chino ordered that Guzmán be dressed in a striped black-and-white prison uniform, like in the movies. He put him in a cage, like an animal, and let the reporters snap away. The monster was displayed for everyone around the world to see. He shouted his

slogans and punched the air. He was less excitable when he had
to take his shirt off in front of the cameras. He was a fat, diseased
old man—he had eaten alfajores and watched movies while the
country burned.

A jail was built on an island a few miles away from the naval
base. After the court sentenced him to life in prison, my men bun-
dled him into a straightjacket and put him on a motorboat. As long
as El Chino was around, there would be no special treatment—he
would have a cement room, a corridor for exercise. Lentils, corn-
meal, vitamin D pills.

On his first day, I could see him looking at the greenery on the
island. He saw the guards drinking soda and eating noodles. He
was hopeful.

Hope is a dangerous thing.

The Doctor gave him a cigarette. I watched the old man struggle with the lighter. He finally got it to work. He puffed quickly,
not bothering to savor it. He just sucked the nicotine in as fast as
he could.

They sat at a table and talked for hours. If Guzmán gave up the
names and locations of his remaining soldiers, there was no reason
he couldn't have a nice retirement out on the ocean. Yes, there had
been humiliation in front of the press, but it was necessary, the government had won the war and had to regain legitimacy. But certainly they could now speak like gentlemen?

It was difficult for me to watch. I almost got up and puked. But
I stayed put. The Doctor knew what he was doing.

As night fell, the Doctor stood up.

"Think about what I've said. I'm sure that after one night in
your cell, living like the proletariat, you'll be more reasonable." He
winked.

I sat beside him on the boat as we sped back to the base. Droplets of water sprayed us.

"If he talks, will he get all the privileges that you promised him?"

"Maybe for a few days."

"We should execute him. There's no sense in keeping him alive."

"The president has spoken . . ."

"Accidents happen. He couldn't blame us."

The Doctor chuckled. He wiped some of the water away from his face.

"We've captured a man who went to war with us for twelve years. He killed seventy thousand people, almost took over the country with some fucking students. The amount of information he must have . . . he's not just a prisoner. He's a resource."

Some resources, I wanted to say, aren't worth the air they breathe.

At dawn the next morning, the head of security on the island radioed. If we could go back as soon as possible—the terruco was ready to speak with us.

—

The highlands

I try not to go down to the village in the evenings. Sometimes I have no choice—I get a call for backup from the policemen, or I need something from the store.

I want an Inca Kola. I haven't had one in weeks. My dinner today consists of bread and stewed tomatoes. Water alone won't do the trick.

I go down the hill and buy a bottle. On my way past the square, I see a man shouting at a little brown dog. His buddy is laughing, sitting on a wall, having a drink.

The man can't be more than a few years younger than me. Nothing better to do than scream at an animal?

I turn away, heading out of the village. Then, I hear a yelp.

The man has kicked the dog. His friend is really laughing now. The dog whimpers and tries to escape. The man follows him, starting to bend down, getting his arm ready for a beating.

I reach him quickly. My bottle shatters. I put the man on the ground. His friend runs away.

I hold his neck against the cobbled stone. He gasps, kicking his arms and legs, trying to pry my fingers from his neck. I use my free to hand to take off my belt.

As soon as I let go, I begin to beat him with the leather. The face. The chest. The hands. He flips around, hollering for help. I start on his back.

I don't know how long I crouch over him. Ten minutes. Fifteen. Maybe longer. My right arm gets tired. I switch to my left. I switch back.

The skin begins to bruise. Some blood escapes from the welts. I can't see very well; it's getting darker and darker. His hollering dies down. Soon, he is whimpering like the dog.

I feel the presence of the villagers. Some of my students stare at the scene from across the square. Parents, too.

Nobody says a word, nobody interferes. There is no jail sentence or fine for beating a stray dog. This is the only way.

I continue until there are no more sounds. He lies still on the ground.

I put my belt back on and search for the dog. I find him settled under a tree, watching my steps. I pick him up and hold him under my arm. He doesn't resist.

I go back to the store and order another soda, and some milk. The owner doesn't charge me. She tells me to have a good night.

With a bag of bottles in one hand and the dog in the other, I head out of the village and up the hill.

———

SHE ANSWERED THE PHONE. I gave her a name, a rank.

She sounded hopeless, tired. She had filed a report with the police, but missing people were rarely found. They were rarely searched for. The process of mourning had already begun.

I reassured her, told her I would be posting one agent at her parents' residence and another at his apartment. Just as a security precaution. She didn't question it.

I left her my phone number. I told her she could call me anytime, day or night. I would be in touch.

She said goodbye. The sound of her soft voice, on the verge of breaking, gave me chills.

I had a lot of time to devote to her lover's case. It would be my final investigation.

The SIN building would be closed down, sold off. The government needed as much cash flow as it could get. We were given a deadline.

I kept my men busy. There was a lot to clean up. Too much information, too many sources. Too many secrets.

The surviving informants were located, rounded up. There was no torture, no ritual. Bullets to the brain, fingertips removed.

Every night we went to a quiet spot along the Rímac River. We heaved the body parts into the dirty water. They mixed with the sewage and garbage—they would never be found.

After removing the physical sources, we had to remove the written ones.

My men and I made the best of those nights. We would wash up with hot water and drink some scotch. In the parking lot, we built a bonfire with some desks and gasoline. One man would keep an eye on the flames. The rest of us would go back inside and fill up cardboard boxes with the files.

Ramfis took a long swig before picking up a stack of three boxes. He walked with me to the elevator.

"Don't know what's going to happen to me," he snorted. "Sit in the house all day. Drink all day." His muscles had become less defined over the last year. A belly was forming. I had always known that the end of the war would be the end of Ramfis.

We dumped the boxes into the flames. No matter how many return trips we made, no matter how much we carried, the file cabinets didn't seem to get any lighter.

We had become hoarders over the years. Paper pushers. Bureaucrats.

Everyone got drunk as the night went on. It was too difficult to purge an entire lifetime of work while sober.

The crackling of the fire was calming. The unease of watching the white and yellow pages turn black slowly dissipated. It was replaced with satisfaction, the satisfaction of steadily completing a task.

There was pleasure in burning the documents, burning every word.

—

The highlands

There are more visitors in the village. Stick-thin young men and women wearing the same skinny jeans, the same smart jackets. Almost all of them are from Lima, but there are some American and

German academics. They give coins and biscuits to the children, they bombard their parents with questions.

They're a swarm, these curious-looking people. They search for the missing, the disappeared.

They can search all they like. I don't think they'll find shallow graves or loose lips. The government is well-liked around here, and the district commander is an efficient man.

When they get tired of the interviews and tours, when the altitude sickness hits them, our visitors lounge around, fuck around, jump into sleeping bags with whoever is willing to share a joint. They even try to imitate the Indians, chewing coca leaves and drinking home-brewed brandy.

I don't think they'll find anything.

My students laugh at them. They stretch out their faces and stumble around like drunkards on my hill, speaking coastal Spanish, imitating the intoxicated pseudo-detectives. I laugh with them.

The visitors are boisterous. They move without a trace of self-doubt or self-awareness. They don't care if they are liked, if they are a nuisance.

I have run into some of them. A drowsy woman will catch my eye when I'm running in the morning—a wobbling man will extend a hand and try to speak to me when I'm buying groceries in the village. Whatever they want, whatever gap they are trying to fill in their hearts, I keep my distance. I offer a cordial nod, I point at my watch. I do nothing, say nothing.

They're unwise to feel so free. Even in peaceful times, even when you can walk around your country again and speak above a whisper, it's a good thing to be careful.

I ASKED IF I COULD GO OVER to the apartment for an interview.
She agreed.

I took sleeping pills the night before. I wanted her to see a
rested face.

The doorman knew who I was. He didn't say anything. I went
upstairs and knocked.

She didn't ask who it was. She opened the door quickly. I held
out my hand.

Her touch was cold. She wore jeans and a sweater. Her hair was
curly—she hadn't bothered to straighten it for weeks. She hadn't
put on makeup—her skin was pale, she had rings under her eyes. I
could smell rosewater, lavender soap.

As I looked at this beautiful young woman, who I was, who I
had been, no longer existed.

She led me inside. I sat beside her on the couch, pulled out a
notebook and a recorder. I asked some generic questions. She answered easily, she had already told the police all of these things.

I could feel her watching me as I wrote.

The question about fidelity was uncomfortable. I could feel
her draw away from me. She dismissed the possibility. He had not
gone off with another woman. It wasn't his character.

Doubt had crept into her voice. Was there a chance that he had
simply gone off to be alone?

She rubbed her eyes, like a child staying up past her bedtime.
"I don't think so."

Was he a solitary man? A secretive man?

She hesitated. "Yes."

Those qualities had attracted her. Since he had pursued her
in the university, she had never had his complete attention. She
liked this. She liked that he had such a rich private world. He was

entertained by his thoughts and his books. His long strolls, a good bottle of wine. He was dark, brooding, but also very predictable.

He went inside himself. He disappeared from the world. But he was not unfaithful. From the day he laid his eyes on her, he had not even looked at another woman.

"If he wanted time alone, he would have said so. He knows I understand him."

She wrapped her arms around herself. Floor heaters were running at full blast, but she was still cold. I imagined her legs under the jeans, the soft stomach and breasts beneath her sweater. Or was it *his* sweater?

She closed her eyes and breathed deeply. "You wear the same cologne as he does."

I put the pen down and looked at her. I gave her a half smile. She almost completed it.

We went over some more things before I stood up to leave. I encouraged her to get back to her normal schedule.

"Are you studying? Working?"

"I take classes at the Catholic University."

"Wonderful. It's important for you to keep busy. Go back to class, be around people."

She touched her curls as she opened the door. "Are you a psychologist?"

I ignored the remark and gave her a gentle pat on the shoulder. I stepped out into the hallway and started walking to the elevator.

She followed me. "Why would someone hurt him?"

Her eyes narrowed at me, concealing vulnerability with anger.

"You don't need a reason to hurt someone."

—

El Chino stopped seeing us so frequently. He moved from the bunker back to the official residence. The war had been all that had occupied his mind for more than two years. The economy, the education system—other things needed his attention.

I met him in his study to give him a briefing. The desk was covered in crumpled papers of different colors and sizes.

He apologized as he pushed some out of the way to make space for my file. He was heavier, tanned. The lines around his mouth had become defined from so much smiling.

"These are the notes that people give me on the street. If I don't go through them every day, they start to pile up."

I had seen him receive these thoughts and pleas. Whenever he toured the provinces and the slums, the citizens reached out to him—he took their hands, put his ears to their mouths. He absorbed their energy as he hiked through the country.

Looking at the notes, I could see that he had an appetite to understand their most intimate concerns. It was endearing, but also dangerous. It made the job too personal, too emotionally charged.

He cleared his desk and folded his hands. "Let's hear the briefing."

The technocrat had returned. I read to him, wondering who would take my place when I was gone.

After reporting to the president, I went to the big cathedral a few blocks away from the Government Palace.

The catacombs under the cathedral had been reopened to the public and the tours had resumed. Archaeology students wore lanyards and offered services in English, French, Portuguese, Italian, German, Japanese. They worked for tips. Vendors and photographers milled around. The beggars on the steps competed with pigeons for food.

I could see the courtyard from the entrance of the church. The monks had been moved out. Gifts shops and snack stands had taken their place.

I ignored the offers of a museum tour and entered the church. I tilted my head back to look at the magnificent ceiling. It was so far away.

It was pointless to wait for silence. Over the din of hushed voices, I tried to take in the restored paintings and glass. Spanish angels stood over Indian demons, touting rifles and gold as they made their way to the heavens.

It was difficult to concentrate. I wondered if mass was held anymore, given the endless circulation of people. Was there even a priest?

I pushed the thought away. I had never confessed. And I never would.

I put all of my change in the donation box. I said a silent prayer and lit a candle.

She wasn't seeking support from her parents or her friends. She hunkered down in the home they had shared, barricading herself away from the world. The doorman bought her groceries.

I visited her. She didn't let me in. I returned a few days later. She opened the door.

She had some legal problems. The writer's brothers had found out that he had gone missing. They were all abroad, but they had hired lawyers. They wanted the apartment, the money in his bank accounts. He had no heirs, she was not his wife.

I promised that I would take care of this. Within a day, the lawyers stopped calling her and dropped all claims in the court. If he wasn't coming back, it was only fair that she inherit what he had left behind.

She was thankful to me. She served me coffee, put out some cake.

"I can have a policewoman accompany you whenever you want to get some fresh air. It's not healthy to stay cooped up like this."

She sipped her coffee and inspected my face. I had known her for so long, but to her, I was basically a stranger. Yet, whenever she gave me her attention, it was like she knew me. She saw me.

As time passed, other phone calls began. Agents, publishers, professors, journalists, critics. They all wanted a piece of him. By association, they wanted a piece of her.

She didn't want to reflect on his legacy when she still couldn't accept that he was gone. She didn't want to be his widow. She didn't feel qualified to discuss his work. She didn't want his ghost to live through her.

I changed her house number. In the last envelopes that we sent out from SIN, I earmarked some payments for the culture editors and book reviewers. The stories on the disappearance dwindled to a more manageable level.

She finally went to see a psychiatrist. He gave her sedatives to stop the panic attacks and help her sleep. She started going for walks again. Lima had never been safer.

It was impossible for me to express what I felt. I waited for her to take the first step.

It happened on one of my visits. I offered her a ride to the university. She accepted.

The car wasn't mine. It was a black sedan. Leather seats, spotless. The kind of car that a detective works an entire lifetime to drive. She made herself comfortable in the seat. She was used to these cars. She was used to being comfortable.

Her energy was better. She had put on some eyeshadow. A black skirt, a stylish coat. Her long curls fell down her back, still damp from the shower. She had stopped straightening it.

We drove in silence. At the university, I pulled up at the entrance. Nobody could see through the glass, but some of the students turned to look at the car.

She kissed me on the cheek.

"Thank you."

"I'll wait for you."

"Ok."

She got out of the car, slammed the door. I watched her walk away.

> *The establishment of a commission for truth and reconciliation is the only possible way forward . . . if the government wants to preserve its legitimacy, there has to be a willingness to accept impartial investigation.*

There was a need for a post-mortem. It was healthy for the country to go through an autopsy. It was beneficial for Peru to take a good long shit.

The Doctor disagreed. He wanted to stop the academics and rogue prosecutors from conducting interviews in the provinces. The terrorism was over, or at least neutralized, that was what mattered.

There was the realization that we would not be in control forever. We had to hide what we could while we still had power. Too much had been done to turn a blind eye and walk away unscathed.

The Doctor argued against the decision—we sat in the room for more than an hour listening to his case. The president was unmoved: he would allow for an investigation. He would call us off. His administration would lose credibility abroad if he cracked down.

I had never seen the Doctor like this. He rubbed his hands to-gether, bounced his knee. Restless. Under the glare of the white light, El Chino was calm.

"I will always protect my men."

And when you're gone, Chino? When you ask for a third term, when they carry cartoons of you in the street, with your gray glasses and pursed lips, with your stiff suits and stiff jaw, and when they scream that they want you to go, will you still protect us? When your people remember to be ungrateful, when you have run out of men to buy, when they rush you to the airport, when only Japan will take you, will you protect us then?

The Doctor rubbed his hands and bounced his knee and I said nothing.

I took her to the bistro beside Kennedy Park. It was her first time back since the day of the explosion.

It was in the evening. The cafés and restaurants were full. We sat outside.

She was nervous. A little down. But she put on a brave face, hiding her grief, wanting to be happy again.

I squeezed her hand. She smiled tightly. Her eyes watched the people passing by. As she sipped her espresso, I could tell that she was trying to hear the conversations at other tables. She was curi-ous, alert. I let her be, I didn't say much.

I ordered her a tall cup of cream and strawberries. The waiter presented it with a flourish. The mound of fruit and cream was generous—no more shortages. I thanked him and ordered an-other coffee.

She stared at the dessert apprehensively. I took a bit of cream with my fingertip and tapped her nose. She was surprised by this act of intimacy. I was worried that I had overstepped, but after she wiped the cream from her nose with a napkin, she smiled at me, a proper smile. She plucked a strawberry and held it to my mouth. She giggled as I took it with my teeth.

"Share with me," she whispered.

Our bites were unhurried. A man strolled by with a little guitar. He strummed for a while, sang in his baritone. I gave him a tip. He played some more, not taking his eyes from her the entire time. Her cheeks reddened. She clutched my hand.

We finished the strawberries and cream. I ordered another. She was enthusiastic at first, eating hungrily, making up for her days of poor appetite. Then, without warning, she slowed down. She watched me eat and drink, stroking my hand, my knee. She was trying to pull me closer.

I called to a vendor who was selling roses. I bought her one. She held it to her nose. She enjoyed how I looked at her. Everything she did was touching.

"Do you want to walk through the park?" I suggested as I paid the bill.

She shook her head. "Let's leave."

We went back to her apartment—their apartment. She opened a bottle of red wine. She poured me a glass before going to the bedroom. She wanted to change her clothes; she'd been wearing the same outfit all day. I sat in the living room and drank, looking at the titles on the bookshelves, enjoying the smell of leather and oak.

The dress matched the color of the wine. It was dark and rich, hugging her curves. Her breasts spoke to me, her bum was defined. She lowered the light and settled down beside me. She crossed her legs and poured herself a glass.

Now I was able to look without discretion. I made a meal of her with my eyes, drank her in like the wine.

After a few minutes, she put the glass down on the coffee table. I massaged her shoulders. She closed her eyes. I pulled one strap of her dress down, then the other. Her skin had become pale.

I kissed her bare thighs, her hands. I slowly went up her neck, making my way to her stained lips.

How long I had waited for this.

We spent some days in the apartment. On other days, I booked a room in a nice hotel. We would swim in the pool, hold each other. Order room service. Stay in bed all night, hardly sleeping.

There was a lot of silence between us. Comfortable silence. I couldn't tell her very much about my life, and she hadn't lived for very long.

She would read a lot, curled up in the sheets. I would join her. I hadn't read with so much pleasure in years. It felt good to start again.

I would buy the newspaper. We would share it. I was drifting away from politics, and preferred to read about the arts. She, on the other hand, was anxious to learn more about the situation at home and abroad that she had ignored for so long. It made it easier to divide up the sections.

We never spoke about him ever again. The investigation was over, the file was burned. I knew that her parents were still searching for answers, especially her mother. But she didn't lift a finger to help.

"How can you accept that the person you shared your life with—how can you accept that he just goes away?"

"You didn't care about him before."

"Well, we care now. Your father cares. I care. But you, you . . ."

"I can't live like this. I can't think about him every day. I don't *want* to think about him every day."

"The police, what have the police told you?"

"Nothing."

"And the man you know? The man you see?"

"He's done all he can do."

"Has he really? Is he a good man? Because these men . . . I don't know. I don't know if they're any good."

"Mamá. Nobody's good in this country. Don't you know that?"

Sometimes she talked in her sleep, or would lock herself in the bathroom to cry. This was understandable, but it happened less and less frequently. The psychiatrist was helping.

"I'm getting better. I'm feeling better."

"You have all the time in the world."

Overall, she seemed normal. Everything was done with the same leisurely care. She glided through her classes, she fell into my arms. Sex was the constant of her days—she wanted it in the mornings, in the nights. She would become irritated if we didn't arrange a meeting in the middle of the day.

I made love like a new man. I did everything to her, everything her heart desired, things I had never contemplated before. She consumed me, debilitated me. I gave up exercising. I devoted myself entirely to pleasuring her.

No matter how much love we made, she demanded more. This excited me and frustrated me at the same time. I treated her more roughly, I hit her, I put my hands around her throat. I hated causing her pain, but I did it anyways to make her happy.

We stopped using the bed or the shower and took to making love on the floor, on the balcony. She liked being in pain, she didn't care if anyone saw her.

She enjoyed it when I took her from behind in front of a mirror. She enjoyed watching herself, watching us.

In the early hours of the morning, we would crumple into each other's arms, exhausted. I would bury my face in her curls and breathe deeply, intent on remembering her smell forever.

I held her in the bed. She was half asleep. I was thirsty. As I thought about getting up for some water, the wailing of sirens broke the silence of our room.

She jumped up, now fully awake. She gasped for air, struggling to hold my body tightly.

"What's wrong? What's wrong?"

There was fear in her voice. She trembled as she tried to restrain her screams. I sat up in the bed and put my arms around her. I stroked her hair, her arms.

"Nothing to worry about. Go back to sleep."

The sirens were not triggered by an explosion. No tremor shook the room, nobody called me. Whatever emergency had taken place, it wasn't a bomb.

She wasn't pacified by my calm. I had to keep holding her, whispering to her. Terror had taken over. I wrapped her naked body in mine and began to kiss her gently, without any of the force that she was so fond of.

"Everything is going to be ok."

I could understand her fear. I could understand it, but I could not feel it.

—

The highlands

The dog never leaves my side. I have not given him a name, but he knows that I am his owner. His best friend.

The children love him. He is a distraction during lessons. I have to tie him to a tree outside the command post. He whines about it, but I have no choice. I leave him with a bone and an apology.

Some of my students look after him when I take the reservists through their routine. I've stepped up the training program—the government wants to boost civil defense. The dog can't keep up, he's too small. The kids play with him on the hill until I return.

The rainy season has begun. Mud slides down the mountains, wiping away entire towns. The village, for the most part, is secure. We've reinforced the nearest contention walls with rocks and nets. The shamans have burned incense and said prayers. There's not much more we can do.

I rise earlier and earlier and sleep later and later. I enjoy the cold nights and mornings too much to waste them away in bed. I take long naps in the afternoons to recover sleep. Sometimes I dream of her touch, her voice.

Sometimes I wish she could be here with me.

I heard it on the radio. News that you know will come, news that you hope you won't hear.

They caught the Doctor in Caracas. He was there on a personal trip, trying to buy himself an exile.

The Venezuelans didn't find his offer generous enough. So, some cops pulled over his convoy. They bagged hundreds of videotapes—he was keeping them in the trunk.

The Doctor liked to watch. Every bribe, every negotiation, every interrogation. He liked to get himself on camera. With company, if possible.

The prosecutors won't get every tape. And what they do get may be partially damaged. But it will be enough. TV stars, publishers, judges, colonels, congresspeople. Just a few hours of film will play life sentences before the country's eyes.

The attorney general has gone rogue. He thinks he can lock the Doctor up in a cage.

I step outside the cabin to finish washing my clothes. I squeeze the shirts, draining them of cold water. I clip them to the string; they can dry in the sun. And suddenly I trip, I fall, I bring the clothes and string down with me, onto the grass. My arms feel heavy, my legs won't cooperate. I can't get up. I can't breathe.

They arrested an untouchable man.

If they caught him, they can catch any of us.

Will they dare put him on trial? If they do, will he dare speak? Will he admit to the death squads, the wiretaps, the torture? The fortunes spent, the innocents lost?

They didn't fight our war. They will never understand it, no matter what he explains.

Will he give them my name? Are there survivors who will remember my face? Will they chopper into this province, climb up my hill, take me when I'm teaching, when I'm sleeping?

So few people know that I exist. So few know my real name. But a few is too many. It would only take one.

I can still hear static coming from inside the cabin, the volume is high. They want to put the Doctor away, maybe in the prison he built for Guzmán. It's sick. It's crueler than anything we ever did.

And what does El Chino say about this? The president has slipped out of Peru, to an international summit. He can't be reached.

I roll onto my back, blinking in the light, trying to see again. You can't feel trapped in the mountains. There is only air, the thinnest air.

One cigarette a day is all I need now. I smoke Incas. The store doesn't have any other brands.

I usually save it for the evening as I watch the sun go down. I sit on the ground with a cup of coffee and smoke while the dog eats his dinner beside me.

I hear someone. The sound of footsteps on the dead leaves.

It's one of my students. She shouts to me and waves. I wave back and put out the cigarette, worried that she'll see my bad habits.

She's climbed all the way up the hill. It's almost dark.

She smiles and sticks out her hands. She is holding a tin container. Food, from her mother. For me.

I take the box and thank her. She crouches down to pet my dog. He wags his tail, barks good-naturedly at her. She gives him a good rub under the chin. He pants happily, enjoying the attention.

I snap off the cover and look inside the box. Green rice and chicken. Some roasted corn. Sweet potato. It smells good. I won't have to cook tonight.

She stands up and stretches. Under her wool cap and above her poncho, I can see her round face peeking out, smiling at me.

"Thank your mother for me, ok?" I give her a hug.

"I will."

"Thank you for bringing me this."

"You're welcome."

"Can I walk you down the hill?"

She shakes her head. She's very independent. "I'll be fine."

"Alright. I'll stand at the head of the path and keep an eye on you instead. Sound good?"

She nods and blows me a kiss. I catch it in the air. She laughs.

I keep the container in my hand, away from the dog's eager grumbling. I walk the few feet with her until she's heading down the path. I stay planted there, watching until she disappears from sight, listening for any disturbance. There is none. She gets back home safely.

The light is disappearing. I decide to smoke another cigarette until the sky is completely dark. Then I'll go inside and eat my dinner.

The tobacco is heavy and sweet. I actually prefer the unfiltered Incas—there's more taste, more smoke. I enjoy every puff, taking my time until there is nothing left but a stub and a burning ember.

I look up. The gray skies of Lima are far away. Here, you can see the stars at night.

There is no place I would rather be.

I keep the radio off; I've stopped listening to useless noise. I don't have a phone or a TV. Newspapers never make it to the village. I have no way of knowing what's going on. Nobody can get in touch with me to deliver a warning.

Whatever comes, whatever happens, I won't be surprised. I won't be afraid.

Waiting isn't living. And so, I wait for nothing.

三

UPRISING

At the presidential palace, security doesn't even bother minding the press corps anymore.

That makes my life a lot easier, dear readers.

The ministers standing around can't wait for the transfer of power. On hushed calls on their new cellphones, they're looking to cash in on their titles and find new jobs in banking or TV. The younger ones want to go to DC, New York, London, Brussels, maybe get their PhDs before they get some of that development money. They'll earn ten times more than in the public sector.

Long before President Fujimori ran off to Japan and resigned, our economy was slowing down and tax revenue was in a free fall. The good times were over. El Chino wasn't motivated to collect from people who weren't motivated to pay up. So, no one bothered, and now the coffers are empty.

Was anyone surprised when the news broke about how much he spent last year? He had to pacify the protesters. He had to throw cash transfers at the elderly. He had to buy up all that food from the

farmers and sell it to the popular markets dirt cheap. He had to pay
all those bastards that the intelligence agency still has on the payroll.

One of our dead writers liked to say, "Peru is a beggar sleeping
on a bench made of gold." It's a cute phrase, but it's not really true.
There's hardly any gold left, and none of us get much sleep.

APRIL 8, 2001

All of my friends left years ago. But where is a journalist to go? You
can't stray too far from your subject matter.

Ex-presidents like Alan García—freshly returned from exile,
after escaping the country he ran into the ground—also don't have
any friends left. He has elders, mentors, confidants, subordinates,
but no friends.

Alan acts like he doesn't have any competition in the upcom-
ing election. Toledo, the little cholo? Lourdes who? He towers over
them in the debates; his girth fills the screen, pushes them aside.
He's dyed his hair some, but it's still thick; he's swapped his leather
jackets for tailored blazers.

Alan has no interest in talking about polls or public policy—he
has no interest in governing. He's just a magnificent speaker who
enjoys the tease of the campaign. He lights up in the throbbing
crowds. He savors the optics when the peasant women hold beer
and fried guinea pig to his nose.

I get a good look at his appetite during the dinner held by the
Peruvian Press Council. Picture it, dear readers: I observe from a
distance as he finishes every dish they bring out, heaping praise
and hot sauce on everything. His white face slowly reddens as he
tears off his tie and his suit jacket, unbuckles his belt and rolls up
his sleeves. The food makes him sweat. He cracks joke after joke,
laughing at the Samurai's midnight flight to Japan, demonstrating
how big the women's breasts are in Chincha. He recounts how,

during his long exile, the only people who gave him good service in French restaurants were the Latin American waiters.

I fall deep under Alan's spell, feeling open to the idea of Peru being led by him again, until I gag on hatred like reflux in my throat. He made my mother and I live through the blackouts, the lines for food, the desperate calculations to stretch the worthless money she worked two jobs for. The four locks on our door. Sendero.

I stop eating and leave my drink half full. He's almost close enough for me to touch. I consider his monstrous body. But there is nothing there to resent. He's the embodiment of the joy of living, a giant created by all of us. Alan dunks a fresh piece of meat in yellow sauce. He slurps some wine to wash it down. His eyes are watery from the spices when he looks at me and smacks his lips.

Dear Alessandra,

My name is Ximena Orozco Orozco.

My two last names are the same not because my parents
are cousins, or because of some coincidence. My father
did not recognize me, and because of the horrible laws
in this country, my mother needed to duplicate her last
name, because without a father's surname in Peru, you
don't exist.

My biological father is the presidential candidate
Alejandro Toledo Manrique.

If you are not convinced of this, I have attached the
reference number that the judiciary has assigned to my
case. My mother has been filing complaints in court since
Toledo entered politics over two years ago. Since I turned
eighteen, I have been filing them myself.

My real name should be Alessandra Toledo Orozco. As
much as the name "Toledo" disgusts me, it's important
that I have it. It would entitle my mother and me to many
things. Money, mostly.

There's a DNA test, too. A judge ordered it, and Toledo
was forced to take it.

You know that there is no real law in this country. You
know that we wait years and years for hearings and
verdicts. It took more than six years just to get a DNA test.

I voted for Lourdes Flores in the first round. I wanted a woman to win, even if she is an ugly old white woman who has never had a boyfriend or a real job. But I found out this morning that she was eliminated. She didn't connect with the poor people. I think only the hard-core churchgoers voted for her, along with a few stupid girls like me.

I can't bear the idea of my father becoming president, but it looks like that's what's going to happen. No newspaper thinks that Alan has a chance, not even yours.

I need you to help me. When Toledo takes power, the justice system will make my file disappear and my mother and I will never get what he owes us.

I've been reading you for months. Even my mother reads you. There is nobody else I feel comfortable reaching out to.

Please read the documents I've attached. Please let me know if we can talk.

Best,
Ximena

APRIL 12, 2001

Every election year, they announce the introduction of new voting machines, and every election, they don't work. This time, it took three days to count the votes.

Lourdes lost a spot in the second round by just a few thousand votes. Toledo and Alan will face each other in a runoff election.

Both men released almost-identical ass-kissing statements, in the hopes of an endorsement from the old hag.

I wish to congratulate Dr. Lourdes Flores for her trailblazing candidacy and her long record of service to Peru. I look forward to meeting with her and discussing the future of our country.

Meanwhile, as the transitional president holds his press conference, the Christian Democrats are filing a lawsuit against the national electoral commission.

I congratulate Dr. Alejandro Toledo and Dr. Alan García on their respective victories. They will face the electorate on June 3, in a runoff election to determine who will govern Peru for the next five years. I have the utmost respect for both candidates, and I look forward to meeting with them in the coming days.

Everyone in Peru is a fucking doctor! We have to call Lourdes "doctor" because she's a lawyer. We have to call Toledo "doctor" because he apparently has a PhD in "human economy" from Stanford—although he has so far failed to present proof of his completed thesis. Meanwhile, Alan—who never finished his undergraduate studies in Peru or France—is Dr. García because the University of New Delhi awarded him an honorary doctorate in the eighties.

I also wish to congratulate the other thirteen presidential candidates, as well as the four thousand Peruvians who ran for seats in Congress. We are all grateful for their contribution to our democracy, and we welcome the newly elected members.

About a quarter of the aforementioned people have criminal charges pending.

The first round of these elections proceeded without notable violence or irregularities. We owe a debt of gratitude to the members of the national police and the armed forces for securing the integrity of the vote. God willing, our second round will also take place without disturbances.

A source in the ministry of the interior informs me that over twenty suspected members of the Shining Path were detained on election day for failed attempts to place bombs in the vicinity of polling sites.

Dear Alessandra,

Have you read the documents yet? Have you looked at the DNA test?

As you can see, I can be just as much of a pain in the ass as my father.

Regards,
Ximena

APRIL 18, 2001

The editorial board denied my leave request. They don't understand why I want to go back to field reporting after I worked so hard
to get a column.

So, I'm still writing something for you, dear readers, as I haul
my ass to Andahuaylas for the love of real journalism. I'm paying
out of pocket to see if there's anything to the uprising that Antauro
Humala is cobbling together.

The taxi driver laughed when I told him where I was going.
But I've been to the interior before. I've been to Piura—but every-
one reminds me that the north is just the beach, all tourists and fish.
The Andes is different.

The taxista argued with me about the best route to the airport—I told him that I had no problem paying extra if he could
make faster time, but he didn't trust me. He sat in silence the rest of
the drive, glaring at me in the rearview mirror, refusing to turn on
the radio. I wonder if he's avoiding the music or the news. I don't
know which one I'm missing out on.

I'm at the airport now. Toledo's on TV, holding a press avail-
ability at the Sheraton Hotel. He just met with the interim president.

After a slow buildup, he shifts into campaign mode. Leaning
against the podium—a small one, which allows his five-foot frame
to be seen—he roughly pats his face with an open palm.

"I'm a cholo, my dear," he beams at a reporter's question about
his ties to a particular bank. "I'm not a Japanese. I'm not a white
pituco from San Isidro. I'm a cholo, goddammit!" He pronounces
"cholo" aggressively, as if he is slurring himself.

I shut the book I'm trying to read and watch the entire press conference. I can't help myself. Toledo has a strange kind of charisma.
Trust me, you don't want to be in his presence, but on television,

from a distance, it's hard to turn away from his guttural raving. It's nothing like Alan García's smooth talking.

You remember his trip to Cuzco, when he got down on his knees and cupped some dirt in his hands and ate it. He actually ate the earth! The foreign reporters feigned cultural understanding as the dark-skinned candidate reabsorbed his Incan heritage. When Toledo tried his hand at Quechua, the locals looked at each other with wide eyes, too polite to do anything else but nod and wince at the mangled words.

Huq simi mana askhachu yachanapaq! he awkwardly shouted, as he pawed the stones of Machu Picchu—"One language is too little." He mispronounced it. What he ended up saying was more along the lines of "One whore is never enough." The reporters left that out of their coverage.

APRIL 19, 2001

On the tiny plane, the passengers are craning their necks to get a look at the honey-colored girl from Lima.

This was a mistake, I think. I should have brought a man. Or I should have brought a white girl, nobody would dare touch a white girl in the provinces—or a chola, a chola would blend in.

I ignore them and listen to music on my headphones while I reread a technical guide about how to work the satellite phone. I need Internet access. I never read my emails, but I want to be able to send reports back to Lima as soon as I write them. It's amazing what's possible now. Internet cafés are springing up all over the city, filled with hundreds of sweaty boys who will sit in chat rooms for the rest of history.

"Bums!" my mother calls them, when she winds around the old neighborhood doing errands. My father had a computer when there were hardly any in Peru; he used it to make charts for his work, and he played games on it when they fired him. My mother sold it the day after his funeral.

We land at the one-runway Andahuaylas airport, which is pathetically small and impressively chaotic. This must be the most action it's ever seen. Every TV channel and radio station dispatched a crack team to cover the uprising. I wear the laminated press pass that an old girlfriend who works at the ministry of public affairs slipped to me.

I'm the only woman at the airport, aside from the cleaning ladies.

Outside, it's cold and humid. I hire a taxi to take me to an inn—I want something modern, or at least clean. I ask the old man which one he recommends. He scratches his head for a while. "Hotel Sol de Oro is good, madame, I think it's the nicest. But I don't know if you want to stay near the Plaza de Armas. There's a lot going on there."

That's exactly where I want to stay.

He loads up my bags and drives me down the muddy road into town. Everything is washed out from the rain. We jolt over deep bumps every few feet.

I ask him questions nonstop. What are his thoughts on Antauro Humala? Does the uprising have support from the local population? What is the economic situation like in Andahuaylas, in Apurímac as a whole? How long has he been driving, is he married, does he have children?

"I feel like you're a reporter," the driver smiles. He answers everything with great detail. The conversation makes time pass quickly, suddenly we're double-parked outside the inn.

Limeños are packed into the narrow street, hauling bags or equipment, hollering at each other under the drizzle. Sol de Oro looks just like the other buildings: low, drab, blue, splattered with mud. The apprehension that I have been pushing down creeps up into my chest, looks around.

"Welcome to the rest of Peru."

APRIL 20, 2001

I wake up in the simple room, with no intention of leaving for a couple of days. I need to adjust to the altitude. I order an Inca Kola from downstairs and eat a chocolate bar that I find in my purse. I turn on the radio—the TV isn't working.

People are dying all over the country. The first cholera outbreak in a decade.

"The engineers from the National Water Authority have issued a boiled water advisory . . . but medical experts warn that it is preferable to purchase bottled water to completely eliminate risk."

For those of us who don't drink tap water under any circumstances, this advice isn't very useful.

"The interim president is asking for patience as his administration negotiates a bailout from the IMF to release emergency health and infrastructure funds . . ."

What about the Chinese? Can't they loan us some cash? They've been buying up tracts of cheap land in Africa—handing out bribes, kicking people off their farms, dynamiting the soil. The Chinese are already in Peru. They'll buy us up too, maybe not today, but certainly under another president. It's inevitable.

I manage to reach my mother on the satellite phone. Thankfully, I left her enough cases of bottled water to last her a month. I tell her about my economic theory. She snorts. "Why not just take their money already, and tell the boys from the IMF to go fuck themselves?"

Alessandra,

Have you ever looked at Toledo's political program?
You can fit it on a flyer, with his party's horrible yellow
colors. His paid workers drop them all over the
slums—they know that middle-class people won't even
bother to read those scraps. If my father wins, just
watch, it will be all those migrants around Lima who
push him over the top, those highlanders can barely read,
they'll just see a dark brown face and go vote for it to
avoid the fine.

I don't know if you've read the police report about the
rape? It was attached to my last email. The rape happened years and years before Toledo was a big deal—we
have the record of the arrest! And you can check with the
ministry of justice—there was never a trial.

Can you at least open an investigation? You have more
than enough information to do that.

I'll be honest with you. At first, I wanted my father to
recognize me. I wanted his name—as much as it makes
me sick—and I wanted compensation for my mother.
But now I want more. I want him put on trial, I want him
charged with rape, I want him to be forced to pay victim's
compensation to us, and then I want him to go to jail. I
don't care what happens to his wife and his other daughter; I don't care if Alan García gets to be president again.
You shouldn't care either.

Many of our presidents—ALL of our presidents—have been shameless. They've robbed, they've ordered killings, they've led and lost stupid wars—you can't imagine all the wars and martyrs we're forced to memorize in school, my God. But for some reason, I think rape is worse. It's something that you can't teach about in school—the nuns won't teach good Catholic girls like me about those acts. If the war heroes raped, if the founders of the republic raped, if any of our dictators or presidents raped—we've had so many, I'm sure at least one of them did—it's not in my textbooks. There are some duels here and there; killing is less embarrassing.

If he raped my mother, you can be sure that he has raped other women.

—Ximena

APRIL 24, 2001

Antauro Humala is holding court in the plaza, just outside the police station. He wears green army fatigues and a brown toque pulled down tightly over his thin, dark eyebrows. He has a flat nose and smooth, oily skin. The retired army major doesn't have a speck of stubble. He's short, but thicker than most citizens of Indigenous descent. He has a wide neck, big hands and a prominent chin that makes him look longer on camera. He tips that chin up and looks into the distance as he answers questions.

I hate how his eyes run over me. They are dark and small, and the gray bags underneath them are substantial. He never smiles—but his squint is full of smugness.

The handle of a gun sticks out of his cargo pants.

His 150 men—all army reservists, veterans from the war with Sendero—have occupied the municipal hall, the radio station, the offices of Southern Copper, the local branch of the Water Authority, and the Agrarian Confederation, in addition to the police station.

Amplifiers, blasting huaynos at all hours of the day and night, fill the plaza of Andahuaylas with mournful singers of modest popularity. The radio voices divide their lyrics equally between Spanish and Quechua.

"The putrid Lima press will say that we are communists, that we are Senderistas. That couldn't be further from the truth. We are simply nationalists—we are simply men and women who love Peru."

I don't see a single woman in the sea of straight black hair and toques. The ladies of Andahuaylas have disappeared—either they are camera-shy, or they want to stay as far away as possible from Peruvian soldiers.

"The putrid Lima press will say that we should simply hold our noses and vote for one of the two candidates on the ballot—one of them a so-called 'socialist' who bled this country dry when he was in power, the other a fake Indian, an Americanized Indian, who, should he be elected, will have a Jewish finance minister sell Peru to the highest bidder."

Some onlookers cheer. The sound of cameras and pens clicking makes me tingle, makes me feel like part of a tribe.

"The putrid Lima press," Antauro shouts into the megaphone, his brown skin reddening, "the putrid Lima press is owned by the Miró-Quesada family, by the Chileans. They do not have your interests at heart, comrades, they do not feel Peruvian at all, they fill their screens and pages with smut, with pornography and racism. We are here, in the heart of the Incan Empire, to tell a different story." His stare spooks the TV cameras, and the red eyes blink back at him, feeding his words to Lima and to all twenty-three other provinces.

"And what about public order?" someone asks.

"There is no public order. Right now, we only have oppression, thievery and lies. This is an action to re-impose public order."

"What does public order look like in your Peru?"

Antauro lets go of the button to wipe his mouth with the back of his hand before seizing the question. "Public order means that Peru belongs to Peruvians. It means that all foreigners—and I mean ALL foreigners, I don't care if they are Chinamen, Germans, Negroes, Canadians, Chileans, Argentinians, Japs, Gringos—are expelled from the national territory. It means that the punishment for corruption, for rape, for murder, for theft—is death."

Hundreds applaud. The men guarding the truck don't blink.

"How will you put criminals to death?" a reporter from Channel 2 asks eagerly, practically rubbing his hands together in anticipation.

"Preferably with the same methods employed by the Inca. By stoning. With rocks that are not too big, and not too small. Death must come, but not too quickly. Every homosexual, every profiteer, every foreigner who refuses to leave, every rapist and murderer, they will be stoned, and, in expedited cases, shot."

A veteran journalist frowns and shouts. "Who is going to enforce such a policy? You? How do you define who is 'foreign' and who is 'Peruvian?' "

Antauro strokes his hairless chin. "If the blood of the Inca flows through your body, then you are a Peruvian. A real Peruvian. The Peruvian people are going to make sure that this country is returned to them, and we will take responsibility for cleaning up the scum that has festered for too long."

The TV men can feel their ratings climb as they shoot this crazy man. Antauro raises a fist, his eyes bulging out of his face. He pinches a line from a long-dead military dictator and roars:

"Peasants! Comrades! The masters will never again feed on your poverty!"

The echo of huayno tunes and clapping hands is unbearable. I push my way out of the herd of reporters, ignoring the looks they throw at me. A few men try to grab at me as I walk past, some whistle, touch their groins. I don't risk swatting them off. I hold on to my camera as if it's protection.

APRIL 26, 2001

I need to file a column, and not much has been happening here. The rain—more like a monsoon—has kept us all inside. So, I'll share something that I forgot to publish earlier.

Before I left Lima, I interviewed a group of Palestinian diplomats at the Arab Union Club. They expressed worries about Toledo. More so about his wife.

"He's already made promises to Sharon . . . if he wins, he'll expel the Palestinian delegation and sign a free trade agreement with Israel. Peru will become the only Latin American country to ignore the issue of settlements at the UN."

"His wife, she's a horror, she has ties to Josef Maiman—an Israeli arms dealer, lives in Brazil. He's giving Toledo millions of dollars."

Eliane Karp is an Israeli-Belgian-American. She and Toledo married in the seventies, when he was on a Peace Corps scholarship at the University of San Francisco. He was studying economics. She was studying anthropology, with a focus on Andean Indigenous cultures. When she discovered an original Peruvian huaco playing intramural soccer on the fields of USF, she immediately made him her pet project.

Eliane gained admiration in the Californian anthropological sphere for being married to a Peruvian Indian. He was one of the few in the Bay Area, even rarer than the Africans that other women in her field managed to poach. Toledo, meanwhile, gained American citizenship, and access to Eliane's family's fortune.

Her shrieking accented Spanish and blazing red hair domi-nated much of the election's first round. She insisted on cam-paigning for her husband, appearing at rallies and panels, until his Argentine consultants convinced him that she was frightening white Peruvians with her rabid indigenist rhetoric. Having a ginger wife was supposed to temper fears about Toledo's skin color, but her radical tendencies actually exacerbated racial tensions.

Eliane is an enigma: a white American, but foreign-born. Jewish, yet fiercely secular. Terrified of black people, and one-half of an in-terracial marriage. She is the kind of academic who belongs to a two-state solution think tank, but is seized with a fit of hysterics whenever someone criticizes the Occupation.

Who can demand that Quechua be taught in Peruvian schools, and still be friends with an arms dealer who sells weapons to Euro-pean settlers in Palestine? Eliane, apparently—she's above any notion of moral consistency. She's the perfect match for a man who gets coked up before he announces his plans to eradicate the coca plant.

APRIL 28, 2001

The Peruvian government rejected the IMF's terms for releasing the emergency health and infrastructure funds. Their team has been asked to leave the country.

The People's Bank of China will transfer the funds to our treasury by the end of the week.

You still cannot drink the water.

I recalculate how long the bottles that I left with my mother will last her.

MAY 1, 2001

I need to keep my laptop plugged in at all times since I spilled Inca Kola on the keyboard. I use dial-up to get online, briefly, before the connection fails.

I need to talk to some locals. And I need a sit-down with Antauro. I didn't come all the way here to settle for his unfiltered rants.

Will he even talk to me? He should. He wants to reach as many people as possible, and *La Prensa* reaches every Tom, Dick and Harry (no offense).

I know that good reporters hope for nothing, but I wouldn't mind if he gets arrested before I see him again.

If he doesn't, then I'll need to be prepared. I dig up some old articles that have just been uploaded online. There are more pieces about the major's father, Isaac, than about him.

Dr. Isaac Humala—still alive—is a radical lawyer from Cusco. He taught at San Marcos University in the sixties before practicing law full-time.

Isaac wants Peru—and all the surrounding Andean nations—to establish a totalitarian state, governed by socialist economic doctrine, and made up of a supreme race of Indigenous Americans. He spent many years in jail as a result of his publications and teachings, before building up a lucrative legal practice. He specializes in representing drug lords before the courts.

Despite preaching socialism and Andean purity, Isaac married an Italian-Peruvian woman: blue-eyed, white-as-snow and loaded.

Isaac and his Italian wife had three sons. They were all brought up with rigorous instruction in their father's Etnocacerismo ideology.

The eldest, Samín, is a Communist Party activist and folk singer. The middle child, Ollanta, is a retired colonel, honorably discharged, now Peru's military attaché in Kobe, Japan—a plum post that has no real duties.

The youngest, Antauro, is currently in Andahuaylas, trying to live out his father's fantasy.

"Watch out for that man," my mother warns me over the phone. "He's a bloody lunatic."

"The human species is made up of four races. The white race dominates most of the world. The yellow race has two major powers—China and Japan. The black race, while being far worse off than the aforementioned races, at least has control over one continent. However, the copper race governs nowhere. We in the Etnocacerismo movement would like to change this. It may seem like a utopian goal, given the constraints of history and centuries of oppression, but unlike the other races, we have the ability to feel, even in moments where everything seems lost, a burning hope. A hope lit by the sun of the Inca, the hope that Tawantinsuyo, our empire, will rise again, no matter how much blood must be shed."

—Dr. Isaac Humala's Theory of Extinction

MAY 4, 2001

I go out to chat with the two reservists standing guard outside the police station.

They're sullen-faced Indians with bandanas tied around their heads, and military fatigues under imitation Nike jackets, zipped up tightly against the cold. They accept my cigarettes after hesitating.

I ask them about Antauro's whereabouts. Would the major be interested in giving *La Prensa* a one-on-one interview?

They take their time considering me as they smoke.

"We'll check," one grunts, but stays where he is. They are used to standing around for endless periods of time.

They speak to me about the price of water, the price of cooking fuel. About the state of the local schools and the dismantlement of the collective farms.

One man opens up a thermos of coffee. They pass a cup back and forth, warming their fingers in the drizzle.

Both are in their late thirties. They spent over a decade fighting Sendero in the Andes throughout the eighties and into the nineties. The scars on their faces and hands make it clear that they endured the most brutal fighting of the war. They survived on instinct while their friends were picked off by the insurgency.

Both of them have killed, oftentimes at close range, with their bare hands. The soldiers and the terrucos alike had lacked appropriate equipment.

"I miss it," one man tells me, exhaling a cloud of smoke. "I miss the war so much, you have no idea."

These men, like the rest of the reservists in the plaza, hail from the poorest strata in Peru. Their parents were landless peasants who benefited from the military government's agrarian reform in the seventies. They are the first in their families to attend school, and the first to speak and write in Spanish.

At the start of the internal conflict, young, unemployed teenagers were recruited from landlocked places without universities or factories, like Andahuaylas. Officers from the coast visited secondary schools across the central Andes, encouraging seventeen-year-olds to sign up and defend Peru from communist guerrillas.

"I had six younger brothers and sisters. We couldn't all live off the plot of land that my parents had. Even if we had all started farming after we finished school, we would barely have had enough to eat."

Healthy teenage boys flocked to join the Peruvian army. The commanding officers—most of them Limeños—wanted to take advantage of their grasp of Quechua and their knowledge of provincial customs. As the army swarmed the towns and villages in the Emergency Zone, these young men proved useful. They gathered information and tracked down Senderista combatants, most of whom were slightly more affluent young Indians and mestizos.

"The terrucos were all rich kids. Well, maybe not really rich, according to someone like you. But their parents were government workers or traders or larger farmers—they were able to go to university in Ayacucho, in Cusco, in Arequipa."

"They were just a few years older than us, they had read a bunch of garbage, and you'd think that they would have been easy to beat, but they were violent motherfuckers, you know? Dead inside."

Those who survived saw between ten and fourteen years of active military service. Almost none were promoted past corporal or sergeant—having not attended the Officers' Academy in Lima, and being Quechua speakers, there was hesitancy within the government to give them more prominent roles.

"What did they think? That, in our hearts, we supported Sendero? But it's true, it's true, even after all we did, some of those top guys never trusted us, even though we were the ones getting butchered."

For years, they put off having families. Many were accused of rape.

"Some guys took advantage, sure. But that's war, that's what happens when you dump a bunch of teenagers into the middle of nowhere with guns. That's what happens, right? But not me, not us."

According to the ministry of justice, more than eight thousand cases of sexual assault and slavery took place during the conflict.

Almost ten years after the war, most of Antauro's reservists remain unemployed. Upon being honorably or dishonorably discharged from the army, they were given a monthly pittance to serve on in the reserves. The military slashed its active-duty ranks following the defeat of Sendero.

"When I came back to Andahuaylas, it felt the same—only emptier. I tried to find work, but there weren't any jobs. And nobody wants to hire a soldier anyways. We have a bad reputation."

"My parents were dead; another family was living in my house. My girlfriend took off to Lima to look for work."

Military pensions—a bit less than seven hundred soles a month—kick in when veterans turn fifty-five. With most enlisted men never having held a job outside of the army, they try to run out the clock, attending reserve exercises, doing menial labor, or meeting up with fellow war veterans.

"Some guys left, they moved to Trujillo, to Arequipa, to Lima— they work as security guards, construction workers, drivers. Some of them reunited with their families. Many of our people left for the big cities during the worst years."

"It was bad here, lady, bad. A shack outside of Lima was better than this shit. While we were far away in other provinces, the motherfucking terrucos raped our girlfriends and burned down our farms."

The occupation of Andahuaylas, led by retired Major Antauro Humala—who served for twelve years in the Emergency Zone—is being done entirely by the war vets. While Major Humala hopes that this insurrection results in a national movement, and while he lists many demands—including the suspension of the ongoing presidential elections, the dissolution of Congress, the expulsion of foreigners and the nationalization of various economic sectors— the reservists express a simpler wish. They hope that the government will re-incorporate them into the regular armed forces.

"There are still some terrorists in the jungle. They work with the narcos. We could go kill them. The government should pay us a proper salary, they should send us there."

"We could finish the job. Why won't they let us? We're here, we've always been here. We're ready to serve. Tell your readers that."

Dear Alessandra,

I don't think a few documents are enough to convince
you (just in case, though, I have attached them again).
I want to tell you the story, properly.

My mother was born in Andahuaylas. My grandparents
ran a supply store.

I know you're there now—maybe that's why you haven't
been able to answer me. Most Limeños never go to
Apurímac province—it has no famous tourist attractions,
no university. It has the steepest mountains, and the
deepest rivers.

I remember the climate from my childhood. It's usually
dry and cool, but around this time of year, it rains and
rains. Just a sheet of water. The altitude sickness is
terrible, even the locals can feel the pressure.

There is no hot Catholic property like in Ayacucho—
there are no pilgrims coming to see the black Christ.
There are a few mines and farms. I think it's the poorest
region in our country.

My mom told me that when she was small, there was
nothing to do. You can probably tell that nothing has
changed: there are no movie theaters or bookstores; it's
all ugly constructions, narrow streets, dirty fountains.

It's maybe the most horrible place and the most beautiful place I have ever seen.

My mom worked in the family store and she went to public school. Thanks to the military government, Andahuaylas was safe—nobody was allowed to bother the girls as they went to school, nobody tried to steal from the shop. But when the soldiers withdrew, there was more and more crime, and the only public college closed.

Then the terrorism began.

My grandparents, being shopkeepers, were the most hated by Sendero, after the prefects and police officers. In the early days, they had to pay a tax for being exploiters. The farm workers began robbing them.

Before the roads closed, my grandparents sent my mother on a bus to Lima. They packed money inside her skirt, they gave her a knife, and they kneeled on the floor of their house and prayed for her. She reached Lima safely, where she was taken in by her aunt.

Sendero would eventually execute my grandfather—they shot him and emptied the store. My grandmother was allowed to go free, but her home was burned down. She would hide with relatives, working on a small patch of land, for almost a decade.

My mother didn't know any of this until much, much later. No mail reached Andahuaylas for the entire civil war. She assumed that her parents were alive (deep down, I think she thought they were dead).

She lived with her aunt in a small room in Santa Anita, where they shared the same mattress. They worked in a bakery together. In the evenings, she took typing and bookkeeping classes at San Marcos University. On Sundays, she went to church and looked through job postings in the newspapers.

She got an interview at ESAN, the business school. The ambitious new dean—a pure Incan, American-educated, only in his mid-thirties—was planning to establish an economics department.

He needed a secretary. A few days after the interview, he hired her.

She doesn't like to talk about it. I have to force her. All she says is that he was soft-spoken, kind of dark and handsome, with rough features. He was shorter than her.

He could have hired another woman. A perky graduate, a professor's wife. But I think he liked that my mother was provincial, like him. He liked that she came from nowhere. He liked that she was quiet and innocent. He didn't want a high-class beauty from Lima who would have screamed for her husband or her father the moment someone tried to lay his hands on her.

MAY 6, 2001

What did they teach you in the army?

To kill. To shoot. To love Peru.

There are many unemployed people in this country. There are many Peruvians with disabilities, without even a reservist's stipend. Why should the government create jobs in the army just for you?

We have fought for this land, goddammit! We wiped out the terrorists, we fought against Ecuador in Cenepa. We have spent our lives defending Peru. Would you have done that? Would you have fought? Would you give your life for this country?

I don't know. Probably not, to be honest with you.

Why not?

MAY 13, 2001

I cling to the rim of the toilet, retching from altitude sickness. I suck on the bitter coca candies that my mother forced me to pack. Yet I find that there's a little more air every day.

I leave the hotel to buy round bread and hot chocolate from a vendor, which I eat and drink on the floor of the room as I type up my pages and send them to Lima. But something is missing.

I walk up and down the four major streets of Andahuaylas—they cut through the city, like a cross—looking for the missing women.

Peeking out from tin doors, they see me. Sometimes they invite me inside.

Many are the wives and daughters of the reservists in the plaza. They spend their days sweeping the dirt floors, listening to the radio, tending to plots of vegetables, reading to their children, walking them to school. There's a smell of damp clothes, of coca and soil. There is not a trace of excess. The women gather to talk, though never for long. There are painful glances at Lima, seen on the few television sets that I encounter. Not for what Lima has—the trashy soap operas, the costumes, the presidential candidates, the manslaughter along the big highway—but rather, yearning for the friends and sisters and brothers and cousins and parents living there, absorbed by the immensity of Lima. Lima is a thing that takes and takes.

The drinking hangs over the women and girls, the drinking that I saw on the drive in from the airport—older men, teetering, intoxicated, boiling sugarcane or banana peels in steel drums. Eyes made red from home-brewed spirits flashed at me in the fog.

When I find the courage to ask about it, there isn't shame or anger—there is only fear. Fear of a beating, fear of no money to buy food, fear of a daughter being touched.

"Beer is cheaper than water in Andahuaylas," a woman tells me.

Sometimes I glimpse a great void, a yearning for something other than a dirt floor and a drunk husband, but a yearning for precisely what, I don't know, because there is also happiness and silence.

I ask myself questions constantly: Is there love here? Or is it just instinct, forming families? Could I ever be happy in this place?

These people share my hue and features, some have piles of paperbacks on their shelves, some of them tall and fair-skinned, looking more like city girls than me, and still I wonder about them as if they are animals, as if they live under a different sky.

They don't know what exactly their husbands and fathers are up to in the plaza, but they are proud of them. They make sure that I know it. With all the Limeños coming to see them, surely that pride is well-placed?

It's not so isolated, I remind myself, when I look at the rusty Beetles in the street, cars that are older than me. There are other parts of Peru that you can only get to by road, by helicopter. The airport is only an hour from here by car—you can pick up and leave whenever you want.

But how do you afford the ticket? And if you can afford it, where do you go? What do you do when you get there?

MAY 20, 2001

We're sitting at a desk in the offices of Southern Copper. Young executives from the mining company are under guard in the next room.

"Major Antauro, why does a rich man—a lawyer and academic— send his sons to a public military school?"

"My father put us in military school because he realized that laws don't change history. Guns change history. And we have the guns."

"Didn't your father want you and your brothers to find your own path in life?"

"Life shouldn't be wasted finding yourself. My father wanted us to free our land. I have devoted my life to that. Not all of us want to be in the spotlight like you, my dear. There's something noble about being part of a group, part of a unit."

"As the leader of this insurrection, Major Humala, aren't you putting yourself in the spotlight? Aren't you the dictator of Andahuaylas, for the time being?"

"I am the spokesman for the Etnocacerista movement because of convenience. Peruvian journalists are too ignorant to comprehend a chorus of voices. The war veterans have asked that I command this operation, but all of our demands have been decided on in committee. There's no personality cult here."

"If the veterans all over Peru rise up and the reservists and the army heed your call to stand down, if the people march to Lima and overthrow the government, who will be in charge? Won't you be the new Túpac Amaru, leading the uprising against the state?"

"You're the only one talking about leaders and followers. You are a reactionary. You haven't bothered to understand what we are fighting for."

"Then tell me!"

"There's no need to get excited."

"A column written by General Aliaga—your former superior— was published in *El Comercio* yesterday. He claims you're behaving in the same way that the Senderistas did in 1980."

"I would be worried if the Miró-Quesada family's newspapers spoke positively about me."

"Denouncing democracy, occupying a town, taking police officers hostage—you don't see a parallel to the start of the terrorism?"

"I fought Sendero. I eliminated many Senderistas during my service in the Emergency Zone. Nobody is going to compare me to terrorists. I won't allow it."

"Why would the newspapers in Lima print these lies, then?"

"The owners of the media are desperate and scared. The nationalism that we represent is incompatible with the special interests of a few powerful groups in Lima. There's more emotion than substance behind their attacks on me—on our movement."

"Are you in favor of a coup d'état?"

"Only if the coup does not come from the highest levels of the army. An overthrow of the government must be led by the ranks, by those with the Incan Spirit."

"You didn't like the comparison with Túpac Amaru, but you've compared yourself to the last Inca in your editorials. Words like 'Uprising' and 'Incan Spirit' seem to follow you. In your leaflets, you write as if the Spanish empire is still around today; you write about ethnicity, purity, about Hitler and Hirohito. What century are you living in? By reading this, some would think you're an indigenist—others would think that you're a Nazi."

"You see, ethnicity is not the same as race. There is a central pillar that you're ignoring—a cultural essence—about what was created in Peru, in Machu Picchu. What was created here is not the same as what came out of the Acropolis. Don't you agree?"

"I'm not here to agree or disagree with you. But the minister of justice has called what is happening here 'terrorism'—is he wrong?"

"The middle-class thinking of the president's cabinet members makes them confuse 'subversion' with 'terrorism.' They have a limited understanding of either word, having spent most of their lives abroad."

"So you consider yourself a subversive. A subversive against what, exactly?"

"Against colonialism."

"Peru is a colony? In what sense?"

"A colony of foreign interests. A colony where the Indians, the disenfranchised, have never truly experienced liberation."

"A colony that pays your brother two hundred thousand dollars a year to be a military attaché in Japan? In Paris?"

"My brother is irrelevant. This insurrection . . ."

"No, no, excuse me Major, your brother isn't irrelevant. Your brother's name appears many times in these leaflets. Your brother—who has the rank of lieutenant-colonel—has written multiple editorials in your father's newspaper over the past year. He's a former soldier, like you. Why isn't he here fighting beside you and your men? Why is he accepting money from a state that he considers to be illegitimate?"

The white office lightening illuminates the sweat on Antauro's face.

"Some patriots still place their faith in public service, in obeying orders. And, in a revitalized Peru, we will need good relations with the rest of the world, we will need an exchange of military culture rather than war. But I can assure you that what we have started here, in the mountains, will eventually lead to a complete renewal of our institutions, and patriots like Ollanta Humala will be essential."

"What does that have to do with two hundred thousand dollars a year?"

"I have nothing more to say on the matter."

"We live in the age of the Internet, yet you—and your father—continuously reference the age of the Inca. Are you really a revolutionary? Or just nostalgic for a time that your ancestors lived in?"

"Our movement isn't retrograde—it's a renaissance. An anti-foreign national revival. We understand that the world has changed, and we want Peru to advance, in the fields of healthcare, education . . . but we still have colonial leftovers that we need to throw away. We also don't want to embrace the worst of neoliberalism and modernity. That's why we are demanding the re-nationalization of our resources, the re-collectivization of land, the end of the monopolies of the Catholic church . . ."

"And isn't it going to be difficult," I interrupt him, "when 90 percent of Peruvians are Catholic? When students are going to school, not working the fields?"

"We want to rescue our classical history, our heritage. We are patriots, we want to do the same thing in Peru that the Europeans and Orientals and Negroes have done for their own people . . ."

"'Asians,' not 'Orientals.' And we say 'African' or 'Black.' We don't use 'Negro' anymore, Major. We haven't for many years."

"Use whatever word you like."

"Words have meanings, the words you use and the way in

which you say them are of some importance when you have the entire country watching you."

"Anyways, while other people throw off their chains, we cling to our so-called 'democracy,' to our plagiarized democracy, our democracy with Down syndrome . . ."

"See, again. Why are you bringing up Down syndrome? Why use it in such a derogatory way?"

"I'm not saying anything derogatory, I'm just speaking . . ."

"No, you're slurring. What do you want, do you want mothers who have children with Down syndrome to leave them in the woods, like the Incas did, like the Spanish did? Are you so obsessed with our past that you want to bring it back to life, with all its horrors?"

"What kind of journalist are you? Don't put words in my mouth. Listen, we're trying to unite our country under a new . . ."

"Please, Major, you're not uniting anything or anyone, you create barriers, you want to build walls between people . . ."

"No!" Antauro slams his hand against the desk. "No! The barriers already exist! We are here to break down walls! You need to understand that . . ."

I repeat what he told me earlier: "There's no need to get excited."

Antauro spits on the tile floor. He takes off his toque, his brown hair is soaked with sweat, his ears are in flames. I remember my mother's words, and I shiver: "He's a bloody lunatic." If something happens to me, please let it be after I upload this piece.

"You're not taking me seriously. This interview is over."

"You promised me an hour, Major. We've only just started."

He mutters something to his men, they follow him out, leaving me to pack up.

—

MAY 22, 2001

What do you want your son to be when he grows up?

A soldier. I think I want him to be a soldier.

But don't you feel betrayed by the armed forces?

Yes, I do.

So why would you want your son to join the army?

Even though I feel betrayed, I still would like him to be a soldier.

You should leave, Alessandra. These guys don't want to negotiate.

I remember the Andhuaylinos, from when I would visit my grandmother, before she passed away. Hard-faced, always watching you. Taking everything in, giving nothing away. Their eyes would follow me everywhere, they are worse than the men in Lima.

Have you had a chance to read about what happened to my mother?

I don't mean to bombard you—I also don't like to write about this stuff, just like how my mom doesn't like to talk about it. I'll never have the full story, but I want to tell you the rest of what I know.

She got hired to be Toledo's secretary at ESAN, and then he started touching her. When they were in his office alone, he would rub her arms as she tried to talk, she would pull away, he would continue with his tasks as if nothing had happened.

My mother met his wife, you know? Eliane. The horrible woman, with the red hair, I'm sure you've met her. She used to drop by to pick him up; she was dividing her time between Stanford and Lima. She used to practice her Quechua on my mother. She had to stand there and humor her, the wife of the man who had begun groping his secretary from behind if she wasn't careful.

I can't believe that she could become First Lady. That bitch thinks we're artifacts. She'll promote Peru all over the world and take away our treasures and dump them in European museums.

Those two deserve each other.

My mother had been working at ESAN for about six months, putting up with her boss's harassment the entire time, when Toledo insisted that she meet him at a famous bar downtown. She refused. He threatened to fire her. So she went.

I don't really know the details, but my great-aunt told me that he put something in my mother's drink. She barely had one or two sips before feeling dizzy. He helped her into a taxi. She woke up in a hotel room, in the Sheraton, just a five-minute drive from the bar.

She cried and cried, my aunt says. I don't know how she cleaned herself up, how she got home, how she found the strength to sleep.

I want to kill him.

My mother told my great-aunt, and she made her file a police report. They skipped work to go to the station.

You might think that the police did nothing—but that's not true. They were actually nice, and when they asked my mother about his background, they must have realized that they had landed a rich Indian. No Indian is untouchable in this country, no matter how powerful he may be. They arrested him at his house in La Molina, in front of his wife and daughter.

I don't know what happened after that—maybe he paid them off, maybe the university got involved.

A university administrator fired my mother after Toledo was released from police custody. He returned as the dean. A few weeks later, she discovered that she was pregnant with me.

My great aunt took care of her. She took her to her doctor's appointments; she massaged her feet when they swelled up.

Neither woman even mentioned abortion. My mother is a super-Catholic Peruvian, the kind that you probably only know from a distance.

For the first four years of my life, my mother tied me to her back. She cleaned mansions in Surco and La Molina during the day, sweeping the bakery floor in the evening. She also sold coffee out of a thermos when she walked back and forth between our room and the bakery.

When I was old enough, she put me in daycare and found a job as an accountant for an import-export business. She still works there. Those Arabs take good care of her. We now own our apartment in Santa Anita, so we don't have to worry about rent.

My mother works six days a week, ten hours a day, and she still goes to church on Sunday. She doesn't force me to go, but I can tell that she's sad when I don't.

When I go to the daily chapel at school (I have no choice), I pray to God that I won't have to work the way my mother works. My friends can't wait to work, they can't wait to get jobs, they see the entrance exams and university as obstacles, but I just want to study what I want for as long as I want, I don't want to have to do anything afterwards.

The elections are so soon. We're going to vote for Alan García. Who are you going to vote for?

—Ximena

"In the developed North, national socialism has the tendency to transform into imperialism. But in the famished and colonized South, nationalism has a profoundly liberating quality. It has nothing to do with oppression, and even less to do with fascism."

—Dr. Isaac Humala's Theory of Extinction

MAY 25, 2001

I go to a bar with the other journalists to watch the final presidential debate. The moderator—who looks refreshingly normal-sized compared to the petite Toledo and giant Alan—begins to read a dozen questions and receive two dozen responses.

"Infrastructure, billions of soles to be dedicated to new infrastructure . . ."

"Credit for entrepreneurs, deeds for the informal sector . . ."

"Unacceptable levels of unemployment . . ."

"Preposterous levels of unemployment . . ."

"Catastrophic levels of unemployment . . ."

"The doubling of wages . . ."

"The tripling of wages . . ."

"Reducing the price of medicine . . ."

"Finally achieving truth and reconciliation . . ."

"Imposing the death penalty . . ."

"Tightening our belts and not being stingy with vital investment . . ."

The answers have been designed by consultants to blandly address everyone. I make myself laugh by imagining Antauro joining them up on stage. There are no interruptions, there are no strange or original proposals . . . I forget who says what.

Address everyone and you address no one. Say everything and you say nothing.

Toledo will win the south, where the Indigenous vote is most significant. Alan will win the north, the historic stronghold of APRA. The wealthy in Lima will vote for Toledo, and the poor will be divided.

Everyone laughs after the closing remarks, as tiny Toledo struggles to escape from Alan's embrace.

MAY 30, 2001

Reporters are streaming past the hotel, shouting to one another, planning to regroup. They're searching for drivers to take them to the airport.

"Something has happened in the plaza," the receptionist informs me.

I begin to run, the camera strap slapping against my waist.

"Miss!" he yells after me. "Stay here! Miss!"

A gunshot. Then another. Then another.

"They're going to close the airport," someone shouts. "They're going to bring the army."

I reach the plaza and stand at the edge, as if looking at a stage, suspended from the performance. Policemen, councillors, executives, engineers on their knees. Hands on their necks. Antauro walks down the line of men, pistol in hand, shooting one after the other, point-blank, in the back of the head.

There are no more flashes of light. I automatically fumble for my camera and begin taking pictures. I put a tape recorder to my lips and click it on. Without thinking, I begin narrating. I count the bodies sprawled on the stones. I count the shots that echo in the emptying plaza.

I am the only onlooker left. Me and the men in fatigues, watching the major, watching the lines on his forehead crease each time he fires, making him look older than his years. He is screaming, his high-pitched voice shaking with rage, making declarations to no one.

I zoom in, trying to capture the finger on the trigger of the black pistol, trying to paint the faces of those who look on.

I stop over the shuttered eyes of the men who are preparing to die.

But I too am being watched. Five or six of the war vets storm towards me. Acne-scarred skin, limbs floating through the drizzle.

I flee into one of the long streets, one of the arms of the cross. They're chasing me. They want me. I'll be ok. The government is going to stamp them out. The major has gone too far. They know it. They have nothing left to lose. They want one last spoil from one last war.

I recognize a blue shack and pound on the door. It does not open. The men arrive. One of them tackles me. I stab him in the eye with my pen, slash another in the face. Someone slaps my cheek. Another kicks me in the face. I fix my eyes on the door.

Women rush out. They rush at my attackers. Screams. Scratches. Their children watch. Soon, the women outnumber the men. They claw and bite, they are vicious, and the war vets protect their eyes and exposed pricks. They can't harm these women. Everyone knows everyone here; they could be the wives or sisters of their comrades in the plaza.

I pull my knees to my chest, I duck my face down, trying to hide in plain sight.

The war vets give up and return to the plaza. The gunshots fade away. Tin doors shut, radios are turned up to maximum volume. A woman invites me inside.

The drizzle turns into rain, soaking my hair, washing over my body. I sink into the soil. I think about the dead men in the plaza, about my mother in Lima. Is my camera lost, was my recorder stolen?

The ground starts to shake. Armored vehicles roll through the streets of Andahuaylas, trekking over the mud, crushing maimed dogs who are too slow to get out of the way.

The war vets flee the plaza in four different directions, some dropping their guns, some continuing to carry them. Uniforms and boots weighed down with water hamper the mad sprint away from their own city, the city they occupied.

The woman is waiting for me.

I listen to the sopping steps; I listen to the exposed wires buzzing above me. The rumbling of the trucks shakes my spine. I taste the rain.

MAY 31, 2001

Thirteen men. Shot dead in the middle of peacetime, in a town where nothing is supposed to happen.

The interim president closed the airports and declared a nationwide curfew.

In the eyes of the world, we're a banana republic again. All is well.

JUNE 3, 2001

A group of officers from the Special Forces picked me up, wrapped me in blankets, and stuck me and my backpack on a medevac helicopter.

These soldiers are different from the ones I know. They are older; their faces are haggard, bearded. They do not wear uniforms—they wear combat pants, olive vests. Black t-shirts in spite of the cold. Bodies without a trace of fat. Machine guns dangle from straps that hang around their thick necks. None of them smoke—they all chew gum.

One catches me looking at him. He smiles kindly. In his hands, there's a worn paperback.

"Where are you from?" I ask him, returning the smile, trying not to feel submissive.

He shrugs. "From here and there."

We're not really allowed to report on these men. We can't interview them or take their pictures or get them on film. They are special.

My hands have not stopped trembling since I regained consciousness.

I'm back in Lima now, back at my desktop. I have my camera and recorder. My laptop got left in the hotel. My mother pops in from time to time to refill my teacup, feed me, or scold me for blinding my eyes on this screen. She complains, but she's never asked me to stop or do something else.

Firefights between the Special Forces and the war vets continue. Most of the reservists have surrendered and been captured. A few remain free on the outskirts of Andahuaylas.

The airport is full of Limeño reporters who tried to flee when the executions began. Planes are grounded. Insurrections in other cities—Tarma, Puno, Huancavelica, Chancay—broke out after Humala's call to arms.

I hope to sell everything to a TV channel. *La Prensa*'s editorial board will be very upset. But it's for the best.

It's taken me a long time to write to you again.

I wanted to tell you sorry about the men who were killed.
But I don't know if you really feel anything for them. Do
you really feel anything for anyone?

I hear that my father is planning to give amnesty to
thousands of Senderistas. I hear that he wants a Nobel
Peace Prize. He wants to impress the world with some
kind of "peace and reconciliation" process.

I don't know why I keep writing to you. I should have
given up hope by now.

—Ximena

JUNE 7, 2001

Special Forces tracked Antauro to a farm. The family sheltering him was killed in the exchange of gunfire.

The government imposed a media blackout throughout the day. All cameras at the Andahuaylas airport were reportedly confiscated as Antauro and the surviving reservists boarded a government jet under armed guard.

Journalists were also barred from documenting the prisoners' arrival in Lima. Airport workers took photos of the prisoners and sold them to the newspapers (perhaps even to mine).

A photograph I received shows that a black sack was placed over Antauro's head as he was led down the steps onto the tarmac. Officers put him in the back of a truck, where he was transported to an undisclosed military facility for solitary confinement. The other reservists were sent to Callao prison, where they will have no access to the major.

The election is over. Alan García conceded—unforgiven by the people, but undeterred, still smiling. President-elect Toledo expressed his continued support of the interim government and confidence in the peaceful transfer of power.

His skin is peeling. He spent the weekend at a resort in Punta Sal.

"Bum," my mother hisses, as she changes the channel.

JUNE 8, 2001

Isaac Humala, at the gates of his house in Surco, addresses reporters, who have been gathering outside since dawn.

He pokes out his long, leathery face and fixes his squinting eyes on the ground until the shouting of questions ends. Finally, he hardly opens his mouth as he speaks in a grating voice.

"My son, Major Antauro Humala, hasn't betrayed his country. On the contrary, it is Peru that has betrayed him. It is Peru that should be ashamed.

"I would like to take this opportunity to denounce the illegitimate government of Peru for selling off our resources to Chile and China; for giving up our sovereignty, all in exchange for a few bribes paid out in dollars. I would also like to condemn our courts and our military, for attacking the men who stand for order and justice.

"My son has failed. But let me warn you, he will not be the last."

JUNE 10, 2001

Toledo has announced that, after he is sworn in, he will appoint Pedro Pablo Kuczynski as minister of finance.

The business community and the financial analysts are thrilled. Kuczynski—or PPK, as he is popularly known—holds an economics degree from Princeton, speaks fluent English, German and French, and plays the piano and the flute. He owns a summer estate in Cieneguilla. He invites the TV crews inside and serenades them with his instruments.

Kuczynski hasn't lived in Peru since 1968, when the junta removed him from his job at the Central Bank. He made periodic trips to Peru during Fujimori's government to help his clients snap up state assets. Some call him an unregistered lobbyist. His net worth is estimated to be in the tens of millions.

He's pasty, old and cheerful, and, despite his vast wealth and his complexion, he doesn't inspire much class hatred. His tragic backstory doesn't hurt. His mother died when he was a small boy. His father, who escaped the Holocaust, was a famous doctor specializing in leprosy. He took his son with him to every province as he treated patients and taught the villagers not to fear people with the disease. He freed them from their cages; he would shake their fingerless hands to demonstrate that nothing was wrong with them

PPK has contacts in DC, New York, London, Boston, Berlin, Singapore, Tokyo, Hong Kong, Cape Town. He will be Toledo's liaison to global finance—so effective that the new president will be able to lie around.

While our Stanford man and our Princeton man enjoy the Government Palace, another Antauro will emerge. The low-level Senderistas will regroup once they're given amnesty and released from prison.

Do you want me to report the story for you, dear readers?

Dear Alessandra,

They say my father will sort things out. I know what that
means. The clients say it to my mom when they can't
pay—he's an economist, he'll know what to do. And,
supposedly, after he's done that, after he's made the
country rich, after he finds the gold that Pizarro couldn't
find, that's when they'll be able to pay off their debts.

People are so stupid, I swear.

I hate engineers, accountants, economists. I know I
shouldn't, I know that everybody is useful in their own
way, but I can't help hating them. Maybe because I can't
graph properly or memorize any formulas.

How am I going to live in Peru, where, lately, numbers are
the only things that matter?

We have a million lawyers, lawyers are begging for work. We
have two million teachers. So, there's no room for me there.

I don't know if you know this, but we apparently have a
massive shortage of people who can actually "do" things.
Every single older brother of my classmates—I'm not
exaggerating—is studying to be an engineer. Maybe a few
are studying business administration, but that's less
impressive. There are fifty private colleges in Lima that
will sell you an MBA if your parents can come up with
the cash.

All my girlfriends who have good grades are taking the entrance exam for math or sciences. I'm the only girl with a strong average who will take the humanities exam. But even if I pass with a high score, what will it matter?

If I get a degree in history or literature or something—if the programs aren't cancelled over the next five years—what am I going to do with it? There's no shortage of lecturers—it's not easy like in your day, when a master's degree was enough. I could join the diplomatic core—but I'm bad at languages, and most of the spots are reserved for the children of diplomats. I could be a tour guide—but most of the tour guides are students who work part-time, and I really hate large groups of people, I hate being watched.

What would you do, if you were me? What would you do if I were your daughter, what would you tell me?

You know what I really want? I want to leave Peru. I want to be an immigrant. That's my dream—to be a foreigner.

Maybe I could get a scholarship to study in Canada, or in Spain. Maybe I could work in a bookstore, or suck it up and work as a tour guide, just for a little while, until I meet someone—not a Peruvian, maybe an Argentine, a Turk?—and marry them and go live with them and never come back here.

If my father's paternity test was revealed—maybe by you?—if it was enforced, if he had to compensate us,

I would give my mother half the money. I would take the rest and leave forever.

I hate that you don't answer me.

—Ximena

JULY 28, 2001

It's Independence Day, Inauguration Day. The dust hangs over everything and everyone. It gets washed away every few days— the ground is always shifting as the mud flows and dries, flows and dries.

The few burly taxi drivers stand around sullenly, watching us disembark.

A councillor—now the interim mayor of Andahuaylas—receives us at the municipal hall. In the long, narrow building, workers have set up white plastic tables that look like patio furniture. We are served guinea pig, rice and corn, blood sausage, sweet potato, red onion salad. They have chopped the guinea pigs up for our com- fort—usually the highlanders just fry them up and eat them whole, working around the spine, sucking on the bones.

The colors of Andahuaylas—the reddish-brownish hues— extend to the food, to the greasy plates of ears, thighs and other indistinguishable body parts. Each piece of meat is traced with what appears to be corroding copper wires. Chemicals in the air from the mines have made the locals nose-blind to the cheap cook- ing oil, the disinfectant that they've poured on the cement. Our eyes cry as we sit and eat.

The councillor and elders offer up their concerns for the media to pass along. A woman serves us plastic cups filled to the brim with homemade dark-purple chicha. It's too heavy and sweet.

When the public officials have tired of their lists, I tell them that I want to walk around. I want to explore this spot, which for so long had gone unnoticed on the exposed flesh of Peru.

Many families have lost a husband or a father to the crack- down. All of the war veterans in the city were either shot dead or transferred away after the failed insurrection. It's the middle of a

Saturday and there's hardly a sound. I see bitter faces, doors shutting, muttered curses. Resentment hangs in the fog.

But the more I walk, the more I see that life has gone on.

The food stalls are open, selling vegetables from the farms, fish from the lakes. On the corners, women fry doughnuts and drizzle them in syrup, selling them to families heading to the plaza. The bells from the main church clang; a choir is practicing for tomorrow.

There are children on holiday, walking around in groups, waving, smiling at the visitors from Lima.

They show me their school. I walk through the empty rooms and see the piles of tattered books. We peek into the new computer room, under the close guard of an elderly watchman, who gets up from his chair to shake my hand.

I see the drawings and cut-out letters on poster boards hanging from the walls. The big windows have no glass; cold air has settled in the building. Some of the children wear wool gloves. Others stick their hands deep into their pockets.

They're proud of their deserted schoolhouse. They find it fun to stroll through it on a weekend, without any teachers around. I ask them questions, they tease me. We laugh and laugh, we run down the empty hallways.

They are weightless, these boys and girls. They seem unaware of what's happened, unaware of where we are. Because to them, we're just living. We're just here.

I take out my camera, snap a picture.

This is the last email I'll send you.

In the polls, everyone says how much they hate Antauro, how they hate what he stands for, how they're appalled by what he did in Andahuaylas.

Do you believe them?

I'm an Indian girl too, Alessandra. I'm not just a Limeña. You may have visited the provinces, but you'll never really see beyond the beauty and the poverty. There's something else in the rest of Peru. This is the land of the Inca, the land of the sun.

And the big men in Lima are stripping the earth and dirtying the water. They shut themselves up behind their gates, and they laugh and drink and sing beneath the clouds of the coast.

I hate the gray skies, I hate the Indians, I hate Lima. I hate the smell of fish. I hate that my grandmother is dead and that Andahuaylas is no longer mine. I hate that my friends all want to be engineers. I hate seeing my father's face in the newspaper. I've stopped reading it. I've stopped reading you.

4

PEACE

HE SEES HER HANDING OUT flyers of herself. The picture shows her naked, touching her breasts, staring at the camera. She waves the flimsy, colorful papers at the men who pass her on the avenue. Most of them ignore her, but some of them stop to check out her body, some of them grab the leaflets, some of them try to touch her and she pulls away. Some of them smile and say dirty things. She never smiles or laughs, she just repeats the words and numbers that are under her picture on the flyer, she doesn't make eye contact, she turns her head and flaps her hand at other pedestrians.

She doesn't see him. He is with the children, they are gathered around him, waiting to cross the road, but she doesn't see him, she has learned to avoid looking at women and children, she can't bear to look at them, she hopes that they don't see the black gel that weighs down on her eyelids, she doesn't want them to see the tight leggings and cheap blouse and high heels and naked picture. She doesn't want to be seen, and yet, she has to be seen, that's the whole point of standing here.

He thinks about this, he wonders if he should move the children along, to a different place to cross. How will he stop and chat with her, when he is supposed to be taking them to the museum? How will he explain stopping to speak with a strange woman on the street?

He feels himself getting hard, just from the sight of her, just from the memories. He tells the children to wait, he doesn't care, he leaves them on the sidewalk and runs across the street, narrowly missing the cars. They honk at him, he waves his hands in apology, curses are thrown, the children yelp and laugh and question.

"Do you recognize me?" he shouts. He runs to her. Do you know me? I know you.

He doesn't know if he says the words or merely thinks them. She is looking at him, the noise of the horns and the drivers has made her look. She is a bit older, yes, but it is still her, the same open body and closed face, the same sharp nose and high cheeks, the same damp hair, the same reluctance.

He thinks: This is the woman I've loved. This is the woman I still love. Why is she here? How is she here? It's like a beautiful ghost, a fantasy, a trick that is taking over his mind in the middle of the day.

She shuts her eyes to him. He sees the purple color, the black lines, the fake lashes. He reaches out to touch her again, and, even though her eyes are closed, she slips from his fingers, just like she always slipped away.

Not here. Not in public. Stay away. Go away. When? He replies. When? He will not accept this; he will not just see her for a moment. He will need more than this, much more.

He tries to put this feeling into words, and he hopes that she understands, and she probably does, because she snatches the pen that protrudes from his front pocket and scribbles the name of a place down on one of her flyers. She folds it and hands it to him.

He can meet her at that café, at four o'clock. She doesn't look at him, can't look at him.

He trusts, he has no choice, and he nods to her and shoves the paper into his pocket, hoping that the children won't see, and he runs back across the street like a maniac, hands extended as if to ward off the cars, he reaches his class.

In the museum, he counts the minutes until he can go back to the school, deposit his students, run back to the center. He finds the small coffeehouse—a canteen, really—sits down, out of breath, pulls out a book, finds his hands trembling, he can't read, he puts the book away. The owner brings a small pot, leaves it on the table without saying a word. He fills a cup and drinks the weak, hot coffee, doesn't add sugar or milk. He waits, he prays, he hopes that she will come, that she will keep her word.

She comes. She wears the same outfit but she now wears a tan coat on top, covering everything up, and she is still shivering. It's a ragged coat, far too thin. She looks down at the table, into the empty cup.

"Do you like working in a school?" It's wonderful that she talks to him without a prompt, without a question from his desperate burned lips. "Is it a public school? A private school?"

"Public. A state school. I teach the elementary grades."

"Ah. So you have papers." She says this wistfully.

"You don't?" He is almost shouting, he loses control around her, forgets where he is, forgets about volume.

"No." She says this like it's obvious, as if there could be any other reason for her to stand on the busy avenue and hand out pictures of herself with times and prices.

Can't she go anywhere else? he finds the courage to ask. Work anywhere else? No, she owes her madam too much money, she has no papers, the capital is too far away, she'll be raped and killed if she leaves, at least here she has a bit of protection. And as she says this they both think the same thing: the diseases will kill her slowly if she has them, the Indians refuse to use condoms, there is no protection.

He orders a hot cake for them to share, she says no, but thankfully the server ignores her and goes to fetch a slice that has been sitting out for a couple of hours in the cold. The server plops it down in front of them on a paper plate with two plastic forks; he gestures that she should eat. She shakes her head but picks at the crumbs.

He remembers the lectures, how she paid such close attention, but how she also fidgeted. Maybe she was fidgeting for the same reason that he and the others were fidgeting—because they had left their hovels after promising their parents that they would study, bury themselves in the books that the elders couldn't read, become professionals, but instead, they were skipping their real classes to listen to a philosopher for three or four hours each day. Instead of getting ready for exams, they were getting ready to follow him into the mountains.

He would hold his piss during those endless lectures about Kant and the universe and then run to the public toilets a few hundred feet from the main building. They were behind a wooden wall that was painted green, the stalls were separated by flimsy flaps, and he pissed, hoping that he would not stumble and plummet to his death. Some couples would shit together, one standing up and holding the hands of the one who was squatting, and then they would switch, there was so much fear of falling in. He didn't imagine that she and the Professor did this—they had their own bathroom, one of the few functioning ones that were connected to pipes. She must have used the tiny one right outside his office.

This was a man who spoke like he had the authority of a God, who could see and hear whatever he wanted, whatever *we* wanted.

He was fatherly and authoritarian, he was brilliant and he was mad. Their parents would not have understood anything he said. Only the young students could understand, because they had been slightly schooled, they had been schooled just enough to be brainwashed. And that's what the Professor did.

"He brainwashed us," he blurts out. He can't help it; the rage has risen to his throat, mixing with the dryness and lust that has settled there.

She blinks. The black ink on her lashes touches the soft skin under her eyes, leaving marks.

"I know."

Where are her parents? Can't she go back to them? He pierces the cake, making it crumble, quickly guiding a piece into his mouth. He chews ravenously, he isn't hungry but he wants to mash something with his teeth.

"They're dead."

"Mine are too. And their land?"

What would they even do with the miserable little plots that their miserable little Indian parents toiled on for decades? They never learned how to farm; they were sent to the state schools and pampered and told to study and given only the lightest chores. Their parents had been more noble than the mothers and fathers of other children, those other mothers and fathers who kept their children illiterate and forced them to plough the fields and collect eggs at dawn, and those unlucky children were now squatting on those abandoned plots, giving little bribes to the policemen. They would never be removed.

It occurs to him that they went to university to learn, but there were hardly any books: a huge disappointment. In the early days, before the Professor, when they had been inseparable, there were classes, but no books, only lecturers who *talked* about books.

They handed out photocopied excerpts, but the rest of the works remained mysteries. And even though the Professor eventually loaned out books—even books in English and French that he had collected during his trips to France, to Red China, to the USSR, to Cambodia—he didn't really like those books, he read them because he had nothing else to read, but they weren't really stories, they were just lectures on paper.

She was picking at the cake; he had a bit more money in his pocket, could he buy her something warmer? She didn't say anything. He imagined that she made more than he did, but she probably didn't get to keep much.

The cake was cold, but it was sweet and good. Her madam didn't give her proper food—she always fussed about the figures of her girls, and it was a relief to eat something crumbly and dry. She hated soup, no, she told him, she didn't want soup, soup was all that she ate.

How about pork, fried pork? He would ask them to make it crispy, he was pleading now, pleading to buy her something. He reminded her of the men who, after waiting for the guards to be out of earshot, pleaded that she come home with them, and she was convinced they would lock her up in a small room, but she said yes to the pork. He looked pleased, he called the server, asked for the pork, handed over some money so that it would be fresh.

"You need to eat something, you look famished." But it was he who was famished. She was a little hungry, but she could tell that this was a man who had known real hunger, he had known it when they were in the mountains together, and he had known it when he had been disappeared, and he still knew hunger, even with his round face and soft stomach she could see that hunger still gnawed away at him.

He's thinking about the village where they were hungry together, one of the first places they took. It was only twenty miles
from the university; the Professor led his willing students on the
hike in the dark. They carried lanterns, for he shunned modern
flashlights. His students carried the axes and knives he had given
them, and he carried a small pistol, it was strapped around his
ankle. The Professor was a heavy man, and old, but he was strong,
he led the hike. She was by his side. He and the other students followed, stumbling over rocks and brambles, pressing against the
side of the cliffs, dirtying themselves.

They entered the small plaza—barely a plaza, a pathetic square,
with a gazebo covered in pigeon shit—and the darkness of the sky
was just beginning to lighten. They walked around the municipal
hall—a modest clay structure with a copper roof—and sat on the
ground, waiting for the first villagers. The Professor stood in the
middle of the square and began to speak, softly at first, then loudly,
then shouting, frantic shouting, drawing the Indians out from their
homes. The night watchman scurried away. Two federal police officers rose from their sleep in the station, and were quickly tackled
by some comrades. They barely yelped, they were barely awake.

It was dawn by the time the mayor appeared. He was tied up,
dragged to the middle of the square. The students ran through the
narrow streets, found the doors built into the muddy walls, knocked
on them, asked for names, dragged people out. She was with him
for a while, but then the Professor called her back, he made her tie
a handkerchief around her face, he gave her his pistol. She stood
beside him in the square, her arms crossed.

It was hard for him to concentrate as he made the rounds and
found the councillors. He kept wondering about her; he enjoyed
how she looked in her long black shirt and black pants, her black

eyes peeking over the fabric, her sharp elbows and legs marking her territory.

They dragged the councillors to the square. By then, the Indians were gathering, at least a hundred of them. They were curious. They could barely understand the Professor—they spoke the language of the highlands, not the country.

It was the end of dawn when they slit the mayor's throat. The red splattered all over his suit. It was easy to see who screamed and who smiled and who expressed no emotion. The Professor commanded the Indians with the gusto of the half-breed that he was. He proclaimed that everything—the copper roofs, the stone floors, the brown bodies, the penned animals, the mayor's wife and daughters—was liberated, everything belonged to the people.

She was calm as he said all of these things. It was as if she didn't care about the mayor's little girls and his shrieking wife, it was as if she didn't care when they were stripped of their clothing and dragged to the middle of the square and made to face the gun.

What was the point of holding the gun? It wasn't as if they could escape—there were too many men.

The Professor only watched for a little while; he led us to the farms at the edge of the village. None of the peasants resisted as we strung up red flags and cut down the wires and fences between plots. "Everything is to be shared," he said. Some older women protested. They were easy to ignore, they posed no threat . . . but the Professor still screamed at them until he was red in the face. He would accept no contradictions; he ordered them to prepare food for us, the liberators.

By then, the screaming from the plaza had died down, the girls' screams were muffled by the masses. Pigs were slaughtered in our honor, quickly stuck onto spits and roasted. The fire engulfed them, smoke rose over the village. The Professor wanted more and more pigs, more fires were started.

He wanted to ask her about the mayor's family, but he never did, he was too scared, he couldn't understand how she had witnessed that, let it happen, never really complained or taken issue. Maybe the Professor would have listened to her?

The Professor took the mayor's house and he took her with him. Some of the other students had taken a village girl for the night, but he couldn't. Not because he didn't want to, but because he was a coward.

"We lived like animals. We went from town to town, village to village. Like animals. Surviving." She says this with exhaustion. She reaches for another chop, moves it to her plate.

As we spread from the villages into the towns, from the provinces into the cities, a reluctance to shoot and butcher was less and less forgivable. The Professor, no longer her master, grew jealous of the men who were around her, especially him, the student who was the least enthusiastic, the least capable, and he decided to dispatch him to place packages. Placing packages is what he called it: delivering them, unwrapping them, preparing them. It kept him on the move; it kept him away from her body. Masked in dark clothing, weighed down with a backpack, he was submerged in risk.

He would crawl under cars, under buses, his face pressed against the moist tar. He would wander into emergency rooms, go to the bathrooms, leave the things behind the toilet. Then he would scramble away, he would force himself not to run, not to draw attention, and no matter how fast he walked, no matter how far away he went, he could hear the explosions, he could hear them ripping through steel and brick and bone and muscle, he could feel the earth shake, the earth end.

No matter how much power your body has over me, he thinks, your body would have been tossed into the sky weightlessly, easily.

He waited for his next instructions. They never came. The Professor was gone, on a trip somewhere, and the commanders didn't know where to send him, there were no packages to be delivered. He was almost relieved, and then, they came. He didn't see them come into the house, he didn't see her. He just saw the black masks, the black shirts and camouflaged pants, the metal cuffs, the trunk of a jeep, a handkerchief pressed to his face, an eye, looking deeply into him, looking red and veiny and dry.

"You didn't come back."

"I didn't come back," he sighs. "But weren't you there? When they came? I thought you were somewhere, maybe upstairs."

"No. I was in a different district. A different house."

There were a few rays of light flickering above them, streaming out of dangling bulbs. He felt the bones in someone's hand press against his sweaty palm as he tried to sleep. He tried to sleep, but he couldn't, he had to keep his eyes open to stop his body from collapsing. He tipped his head and watched the back of people's necks. Men held the dogs tightly, they walked slowly, their eyes roaming, rolling. He finally closed his own eyes, afraid that he would see the dogs, or worse, that they would see him.

Somewhere, a girl cried.

"It could have been you. It could have been you, somewhere, down one of those hallways."

"It wasn't me. I wasn't in a place like that."

"Oh. You weren't?"

There is more silence, only broken by the hum of the radio. The white tile floors are dirty, sticky. The table is sticky, too. He removes his elbows; he has already dirtied his white shirt, he will have to wash and hang another and hope it dries by morning.

"Are you a good teacher? Are you good to your students?"

"Yes, yes, of course I am," he reassures her, practically pleading, "they like me very much."

When he sees his students cry, he wants to hold them and clean them up and comfort them, but he suppresses the urge, he finds a woman to do it.

He's not breathing, he's just looking at her, he rambles and then he shuts up and stares. She doesn't care. She can listen and not listen. She's full now, she should go. Will he let her go?

There were doctors and surgeons and nurses and everybody who had lost somebody to him, to her, to them, they hated them so much, they hated them because they'd taken away their family and friends and peace. They hated their revolution, but they were so exhausted of hate, they did their work without hate, they were too tired to hate, they had so many of them, so many bodies. He would wake up to a tube of water or a pack of matches, to the scalpel, to the eyes, to the fingers on his body. They cut him up and stitched him back together.

"I can't hear this. I don't want you to tell me this."

"But I want you to hear."

"It's not any worse than the things we did. The things he did."

She wants to scream at his stupid flabby face, at his beady little eyes, with his job and his documents and his stories.

He hasn't stopped speaking, he hasn't noticed that she's no longer here. He's talking about how they had to roast rats, how they had to burn their own shit to stay warm in the prisons. They put the prisons far away, in the jungles or in the desert, and at night, either the heat or the cold was unbearable. He doesn't mention the rape—even though it was daily—even though he tells her about everything else.

He's still talking, remembering, reliving.

Nobody ever cleaned the cells, the prisons were all burned down after a few years, they never planned on reusing them. He remembers nothing else, only scratching and bleeding. He went nose-blind, he only began to smell again when he came to this town, when the pork managed to break past the nose's refusal to take in any more scents. He became so thin, thinner than he had ever been during the revolution in the mountains, thinner than he had been when they hiked for days and days. All of the other inmates assured him that his parents were dead. But you don't even know their names! I haven't even told you where they're from! Doesn't matter, they're dead, don't worry, they're dead, just be thankful they aren't in here with you, your parents are fertilizing the land, they laughed.

Are you in prison if there are no guards? He doesn't recall seeing any—you could slip through the bars, wander the passages, step outside, see for miles. You could even slip out the gates—the men in the watchtowers couldn't aim—and walk, without shoes, over the rocks and sand, you could walk and be relieved not to see humans, and after hours, after a day, you would suddenly be searching for the sight of someone, anyone, and you would find nothing, only branches without leaves, muddy streams without fish, grass that became dirt, tightly packed huts of mud and hay that were emptied a long time ago.

I am mad, he thought, as he slipped away from a prison, a prison at the ashy foot of a volcano, and he went back, he went back, he wept as he returned to the cells, he had no choice.

When the war was over, when the last of their comrades on the outside were defeated, when she escaped the soldiers, when the Professor was shipped to an island and placed in a box made of steel, they let him out.

Yes, she thinks, he has the most ordinary face, a face she would have missed had she passed him in the street. She feels nothing for him. She wants to leave the coffeehouse, she wants to go freshen up for the long night ahead of her.

If things had been different, maybe she would have reacted to his advances, maybe she wouldn't have gone to the Professor's office, maybe she would have stayed in the dormitories and studied with him. They would have been killed by the other converts. Perhaps that would have been better, no?

She stands up. He stands as well, placing the last of his bills on the table. They leave quickly together, not saying a word to the server or the cook, they duck out into the street that has filled with bodies, they are jostled, stepped on. He tries to keep pace with her, she is walking fast, it has gotten dark, sound systems and waiters shout from the cement facades, they coo to the evening crowds, they beg for attention.

"Come home with me."

"No."

"Why not?"

"I have to go. I have to work. My madam will be upset if I'm not back by nightfall."

Her madam! This enrages him. She speaks like she's a slave. But they aren't slaves anymore, they are free!

"Thank you for the food."

"Let me buy you another meal, tomorrow," he begs, unsatisfied with her thanks. "If you won't stay with me tonight, let me come see you tomorrow."

"You have classes to teach."

I don't know anything, he thinks. I know barely more than what I knew when I was seventeen years old.

That's why he can teach children—he only knows what they need to know. It's all he remembers.

He wants to start a revolution in this town, he wants to gather all the men and boys, he wants to break into the police station, the army barracks, hand out the weapons, storm the municipal hall, declare an insurgency, lead them through the mountain towns to the coast and to the capital. He wants them to take the mines and factories and shut them down, he wants them to learn to farm together, the elders can teach them, they can clean up all this filth, all this shit, they can stop buying things and grow their own food and live together. He wants to repeat what they did in the mountains; he wants them to do it right

The more the Professor drank, the more he theorized, the more he debated . . . not with them, but with himself. In front of his willing audience, he sustained dialectical conversations, he talked in circles, he drank until his eyes turned red. His breathing slowed, his endless shouts became moments of reflection, and in crept the doubt, terrifying doubt, from which they couldn't turn away.

We are not ready to be civilized, the Professor whispered, pacing, hands folded behind his back. Our history is blood and bone and reaction. We are the children of conquerors and slaves who overthrew emperors and Gods, and then crumbled, became dust. Our people are silence. And that silence is a universe, all on its own; the universe is here, in these mountains. And it must be cut off, it doesn't need to touch oceans or borders, it doesn't need to be visited by planes or trains, it doesn't need anything or anyone else, we must silence it from the world, we are more than a world.

We have the knowledge, but they do not, *you* do not, he shrugged, saying this lazily, without fear. Knowledge makes you calm, and he was calm, he was in no rush, he drank more and more and the pessimism was quenched, he smiled, passed some of the female comrades, bent down to rub his beard against their delighted cheeks.

And some will say that there is no time! But time is irrelevant, we are more than time, we will outlast time. We are not in a moment of history, no, no. We are the consequence of all of history. We are the end of history.

The unbearable energy and conviction returned, his circular speech was complete, the war would continue, happily, unhurriedly. His declarations were punctuated by the clang of church bells—it was nearly morning, someone was still in the church, they still hadn't burned it to the ground. The Professor heard the noise, but he didn't react, he didn't fly into a rage. Instead, he demanded music, and some comrades fumbled with a tape recorder.

He urged the girls to their feet; he would dance, and they would dance with him. He stuck out his arms like he was nailed to a cross, tossed his glasses away, tilted his face up to the sky, closed his red eyes, began snapping his fingers. Taking precise, small steps to the twang of the lute strings, he slowly picked up the pace. The music was happy and quick, the musician picked at the instrument with deft skill, it was sharp and trembling. He shouted, the men clapped, the girls imitated him, followed his steps—she was there, she wasn't smiling but she also stood up, stretched out her arms, shook her body, lost herself.

They were all watching, listening, following.

He was the one who was no longer there.

He hated thinking about those lectures and dances. They meant nothing, they made him sick. She was the only reason he had even been there; she was the reason he kept thinking, remembering. He wished he hadn't seen her on the avenue selling her body, he wished he had never met her. But how could he wish that? He loved her, he really did, she was the only thing he had ever loved, still loved.

There were moments of freedom, though. He felt free underneath those cars, away from others. He felt free running down empty streets in the middle of the night. It was liberating to be alone, away

from the rest of them. He felt free when he caught a girl on the outskirts of the village, he felt free when she squirmed and screamed in
his grip, he felt free when he let her go.

He had fought, hard, for his people, and yet, he hated their
smells and their stares and their faces and their sounds, he hated just
being around them, so close to them, he hated being one of them.

"I don't care about teaching, I don't care."

"Yes, you care," she says softly. He grabs her arm, she tugs
away but he doesn't let go, he doesn't want to lose her in the swarm
of people, she relents and walks with his hand holding on to her,
guiding him like a blind man.

He wants to take me home with him, she thinks. He wants to
fuck me. I won't let him.

They continue through the masses, they reach the avenue, she
stops. He can see that she doesn't want to lead him to the exact
location.

She jogs away, and he tries to follow her, with his eyes, then
with his feet, but she moves quickly, she disappears into the throngs
of people on the sidewalk, she blends into the hundreds of other
girls wearing tight, used clothes, and his heart throbs because he
doesn't have the address, he's lost the flyer with the directions.

She looks so much like the women in the street. For a moment,
she isn't special—she is just another body that he looks at. But the
moment passes, and he wants her, only her.

He'll find her again, and once he realizes this, once he realizes
that she is not lost, he can drag his body home.

He remembers that she wasn't just good at killing the dogs; she
wasn't just good at sliding her slender body up the poles, nimbly
lacing twine for the hangings. She was good in the dark, good with
fire. She was brutal, more brutal than he could ever be. She was

braver than any of the commanders, she ran with the sticks as the flames tasted her hands, she ran over the rocky hills that surrounded the capital, she draped her arm down and touched the sticks to the ground, she drew the sickle first, and then crossed her design with the hammer.

She burned us into the mountains, into the hills, she hypnotized millions of people below. And I saw her come alive as she did this. And as he ran ahead of her, he would see the flames out of the corner of his eye.

And as he runs, she is waking up, sore from a long night, cold after hours of warm bodies, reeking of rancid sweat. She crawls out of the tangled sheets, strips the bed in blindness, flips open the shutters, covering her bare breasts with an arm. She feels small and weak; she walks into the hall and to the bathroom, she jiggles the handle of the door, it is locked, she has to wait. She leans against the wall, naked, shivering, her skin inflamed, her eyes hardly open.

"Hurry up," she mutters. It smells like smoke, the girl must be smoking in the bathtub. She could go downstairs and find another bathroom, but there may be clients who are still waking up, they may try to grab her while she's still barely conscious, it's better to be patient.

The door finally opens and, without looking at the girl who passes her, she steps inside the humid bathroom, shuts the door, turns the water heater and the shower on, lets the stream knock her around.

When the pressure and the heat die down, she leaves, dripping all over the hallway. She closes the door to her room, finds a towel, roughly moves it everywhere. She pulls on underwear, a sweatshirt, leggings, slips into sneakers, leaves her little room, soundlessly goes down the steps and out the door into the murky streets.

She's starving. She goes to buy groceries. It worries her to leave her room unattended for too long. She has sewn her money into the bottom of her mattress—she can't open a bank account, you need an identity card to do that.

I have to save, she tells herself. It will cost thousands to buy documents, to have them forged. She already knows a man who will do it. He will charge more than half of her savings, but it's worth it, it's worth it, he has some bureaucrats in his pocket in the capital, he'll add her to the system, she'll replace a dead person or a missing person. He'll help her exist again.

She hasn't existed in years.

She'll pack up one day and leave the whorehouse. She'll leave in the early morning, when the madam is busy counting her money. She'll go north, to the sunny provinces near the equator. And she'll find work in a hotel, or in a store, near the beach.

She's never seen the ocean. Almost all the people in this country live beside the ocean, but she's never seen it. Her parents never took her, they never bothered; they weren't even that poor, they could have gone by bus. She'll have to go there by herself.

The kitchen is dark when she returns; her madam is eating. She glares at her, they don't speak. She washes her hands and a head of lettuce, peeling it inside a bowl. The leaves are tinged blue with the chemical they use to clean it.

In the north, she'll eat fresh fish and fresh fruit every day.

She drags the meal out for as long as she can—there isn't much to do during the day, other than eat. She can't focus on a book; the parks are dirty. She's sore, she's dehydrated, she drinks glass after glass of boiled water from the jar.

She wants to leave again, she wants to stop being bored, she wants to go outside, even if the only thing she has to do is hawk her flyers on the avenue.

The soldiers taught her the true meaning of boredom after they captured her. They spent years in the mountains, wandering from village to village, not understanding, not wanting to understand, waiting days and weeks for something to happen, and when it happened it was unexpected and painful and fatal, and then the waiting would return and they would wish for something to happen again. When they locked her up in the barracks and lined up for her, there was no conversation. She had nothing to think about for those hours and those days.

But the soldiers also spared her from proximity. They spared her from running into the widows and orphans she had created—who are now hidden but who still live—and they spared her from hearing the mourning that she also created. They spared her from having to walk down the paths full of ghosts who dance, in silence, with the survivors who don't want to live alone anymore.

These thoughts hurl her from the bed, she grabs her flyers and runs down the steps, into the street, her legs taking her to the avenue where she can make more money to go away.

But the madam tells her to stop. Outside, the guards are shouting. There's a man—he's trying to come inside.

He finds the house where she lives, he pushes his way to the door, there are two lanky and pockmarked men leaning against a wall across the street. They tell him to step back, he insists that he is here to see his friend, his old comrade, they don't care, he has to get back, but he insists, *I'm not a client, can't you fuckers understand?* They shake their heads, they can't hear him. They tell him to step back. They keep leaning against the wall, sharing a joint.

He's not going to wait outside with these perverts. He screams, the guards yell at him to stop and he tells them to fuck themselves, fuck themselves and their mothers, he calls out her name.

And the door opens, and there's an old woman, with her arms crossed, and he looks past her, and she's there. He says her name.

Is he mad? He's soaked; he smells of cigarettes, his eyes are wild. And he's babbling now, about how he wants her to leave this place, leave these men, come back with him to his place. It's not very nice or very big, but it must be better than this, it must be, and he promises to take care of her, he has some money saved, in a few years they can go back to the mountains, they can go back. You don't need an identity card there. They can live on a small plot of land and farm, like how their parents farmed, like how their grand-parents farmed, would she like that, living where you could see a tree, an animal? Away from all of this grime, all of these people?

He's right, in some ways. He's talking about animals now, about birds, about how ugly it is, here in this town.

It's been years since I've heard a bird, she thinks. And then, she realizes that it doesn't really matter, she doesn't really care. She thinks about the girls she went to school with, in her little village school. She wonders if she would see them again if she went back to the mountains.

Were they alive? Had they gotten married, did they have chil-dren? And she thinks about their lives and she feels sick.

He wants to keep her in a room, like the soldiers did.

"Go away. You need to go away. You can't be here."

She looks paler and thinner than she did yesterday. Is she sick? All of the girls who work in this whorehouse must be sick, sleeping with so many men.

"Please, please come with me, don't stay here, you're sick, look at you, I'll take care of you, I promise."

The old bitch is blocking his path. Who the hell does she think she is? Does she think she owns his comrade? He once would have killed someone who dared stand in front of him like this, with their arms crossed so arrogantly. He once killed witches like these.

He was glad that the Professor still had his eyes. He could not be comforted by darkness in his cell. The Professor would swallow the vitamins and eat the government meals—the same ones that his students ate back at the schoolhouse—and he would live inside that box for twenty-three hours each day, with only the company of his memories. And he would want to kill himself every day, but he wouldn't have the courage, he wouldn't have the materials or the strength. He was unwatched. He was not among the living anymore, and he was not allowed to die.

This image brings him so much pleasure and relief that he feels wetness in his eyes. He laughs with joy.

"Get out of my way. She's coming with me."

"Please leave. I'm begging you." And she folds her hands! "I'm begging you, please leave."

"I want you to come live with me. I'll take care of you. We'll forget all of this. I want to have children with you."

She shakes her head, resisting, not listening, and this makes him angry.

"Where are your parents? What would they think of you?"

And now she is angry, angry and crying, "Why would you talk about my parents? What gives you the right? Go away, go away!"

And she feels like she is inside the dream she always has, the dream she has almost every night, where she throws her baby from the bus. But she doesn't have a baby; they gave her pills in the barracks.

"Thank God I never had children," she sighs. "Thank God."

And this hurts him. His sadness is overwhelming, but she doesn't care. She says it again and again—thank God, thank God—until he lunges at her.

She doesn't protect herself. She stands there as he wraps his hands around her neck and prepares to tear at her face. But the guards have set upon him like dogs, they've been watching him eagerly, just waiting for him to snap and try to grab her. They seize him, and they drag him out of the doorway and into the street, and he feels incomprehensible pain as they twist and fold his limbs and crush him with their boots.

She doesn't see them. She doesn't see the guards or her madam or the schoolteacher hollering in front of her. She doesn't see anything. She doesn't need to. Because she knows that she will see the sun again. And she will see the ocean.